HERMANOS

Roderic Schmidt

PublishAmerica
Baltimore

ISBN: 1-4137-9149-2
PUBLISHED BY PUBLISHAMERICA, LLLP
www.publishamerica.com
Baltimore

With special thanks and deep appreciation
to Barbara for her unfailing patience
and her close readings
and to Bob for his careful, thoughtful criticism.

I

Dos Padres Valley. Once, much earlier in its history, the valley was a magnificent landscape of native oaks and chaparral, and grasses, hills, mesas, and meadows along a grand and life-giving river, known widely as the San Marcos River. It was alongside this river that the California missionaries had established Dos Padres Station. The Station was the product of necessity...an inn, a mailbox, a stable, all designed as a way-station on the California coastline between the major harbors of Santa Barbara and San Luis Obispo. The station was run, as the name implies, by two missionaries from the San Marcos Mission which had been established in the mid-1700's, first at the location of the Station and then later, after being destroyed by a series of earthquakes, to the hillsides of the Valley almost two miles eastward. Thus, the Station, which officially reopened in 1846, became, because of its distance from and its proximity to the Mission, a kind of entrepreneurial autonomy. And because of its importance as a safe stopover for travelers, Dos Padres grew from the simple, three or four buildings that had been rescued from the earthquake, to a budding community.

And as this community grew, its inhabitants opened the valley floor to a township, and the hills and mesas around and above flourished both as a fertile ranchland and pastureland...as an increasingly important collection of small, productive farms. The Valley was blessed with a river which had over centuries provided its broad banks with topsoil that simply bred plant-life. Vegetables of every sort, fruit trees, walnut and almond trees, flowers, all blossomed spring, summer, and fall along the valley floor.

And the river, the San Marcos River, flowing to the Pacific, spawned trout year-round and an annual salmon run that was unparalleled on the central coast. Deer regularly flocked to its banks as did wild boar, wild goats, coyotes and wolves, and California's ubiquitous mountain lions. Birds too numerous to mention nested in the scrub oak; quail flew low-flying patterns over the grasses and nested their young along the river bank. And the coastal access to Los Lobos beach was a triumph of natural beauty. A single two-lane road led the way through coastal oaks, ceanothus, spring flowers and fall colors, and abundant grasslands, before giving way to a consummate cliff-side approach to the grand sweep of the Pacific. These cliffs, carved by millions of years of tidal activity, displayed all the wonders of nature and her colors—greens, golds, silvers, browns, blues, blacks –

colors which glowed especially iridescently in the setting sun. A surfer's paradise, the Los Lobos coastline remained virtually untouched by the ravages of the careless beach visitor. Surfers, swimmers, picnickers, all seemed unconsciously to understand that Los Lobos belonged not to humans who might momentarily inhabit the landscape, but to nature.

The town grew. And Dos Padres Station became officially Dos Padres Valley. With its eleven elementary schools and two high schools, its small townness was gradually disappearing as immigrants from around California chose the very smallness of the community as their own—never realizing that in so choosing, they were, sadly enough, destroying the very complexion they sought. The river was dammed far upstream, the fertile fields gave way to cement pads, the town itself expanded from a quiet admixture of settling whites, nearly-native Mexicans, and native Indians to a white community that ignored its native populations and segregated its Mexican citizenry to menial jobs and barrio-like neighborhoods. But slowly, an interesting socio-economic element began inexorably to alter forever the little world of Dos Padres Valley: the Mexican population began to rise to prominence – well-educated, upwardly mobile, bi-lingual, increasingly wealthy. Dos Padres Valley was in the midst of a change not readily apparent to its citizens.

I I

It was nigh onto a warm spring Sunday evening. Aron Levin lay quietly on a sandy ledge of Los Lobos, soaking up the sun and looking out across the stretch of breaking waves. A towel drawn loosely about his waist, his wet suit drying in the late afternoon sun, he lay on his stomach, his head propped up on his elbows watching as what earlier-on had been some fine breaking, four-to-five-foot waves dissolve into a dying, wind-blown surf. *Offshore winds'll do it every time*, he thought to himself. He was a seventeen-year-old whose stature had reached a premature maturity—a short stocky frame, one surely given to early overweight; yet, now, he was a chunky, formidable presence as a high school senior. His soft, curly hair, jet-black even in the middle of summer, and his sturdy build, gave off the appearance one who was effortlessly in control of his surroundings.

Farther out, maybe half-a-mile out, a big one, close to six-foot, flashing brilliantly in the late afternoon sun, now curling, held its shape momentarily, then folded in upon itself with the kind of power that every surfer chills to feel beneath his board.

Aron, surveying the horizon, could identify four of the six surfers still waiting to catch one last wave. Two others he couldn't – and this was an intrigue, for Aron liked always to be in control. This stretch of Los Lobos was *his* beach, *his* turf—had been for the better part of the past five years. He knew the lay of the land, the ledges, the places where the surf curled especially fine after stormy weather, the rocky outcropping that occasionally, when the tides shifted, could produce awesome waves. He knew the surfers. These two he didn't know.

Chris Battleson, Aron's best friend and surfing buddy, came off his board at the shoreline and reached back to free his tether, waving at Aron as he did so. Aron nodded, waiting, watching as Chris crossed the beach and leaned his board against the margin of the ledge, hopping up and stripping off his wet suit as he did so.

"That was awesome…while it lasted," he wheezed, shaking water from his hair. Chris' six-foot frame, well-muscled, was tanned from both his surfing and his tennis playing—his two passions. His short curly hair, a natural sandy brown, turned to a sun-bleached blonde each summer. His dark eyes, a startling presence beneath his almost blonde eye brows, were piercingly black and flashed quickly when he was angry. It was an appearance that he had been told about over and over—and he hated the dead-giveaway that his eyes provided to his inner emotions. He stood there toweling off as he stared out at the small waves that formed and quickly broke in the wind.

"Yeah," Aron agreed, "but what I want know is who are those two dudes out there. I can see Geoff and Brian…and that's Buddy out there on the left. But those two…off to the right…who are *they*?"

"Them? You know them. Those two new guys…ones that just transferred from Dos Padres," Chris said cupping his hand over his eyes. "The one on the far right, kneeling on his board's Alfredo. He's in our Lit class, and Calculus, too. And Alfredo's in my Photo class seventh period. You remember? The other one's—"

"Alfredo's a *spic!*" Aron spat out the words, interrupting Chris. "What's he doing out there? I've never seen downtown guys on this part of the beach. And anyways, I didn't know that spics knew *how* to surf."

"Aw, come on, Ari. Lighten up!" Chris sat down, his knees bent, his elbows resting on them, smiling. "Alfredo's okay, Ari…give him a break! He's trying to get along. He even waved to me out there. And the other guy's Mario, his brother. Them and their family moved into the Village…that's why they transferred to Mission. Chris glanced over at Aron whose grim looks reflected his growing anger.

"Anyway," he continued, "Alfredo's actually a good surfer. He made some pretty slick moves out there—"

Aron abruptly waved off his friend. "He doesn't belong. He'll never belong. He's not one of us, Christo. Both of them…they've got to learn. They don't belong."

Chris shrugged his shoulders. "Well, let's forget 'em for a couple of minutes. Okay, Ari? We got to talk…I'm in kind of a jam, and I need to…well…just talk."

He put his head down on his kneecaps, realizing that he was stammering, hating how foolish he must be sounding.

Aron looked over at him and saw his best friend lift his head to stare out again across the water. He'd heard his friend's stammering, heard as well the subtle fear that had crept into Chris's voice. He didn't like the sound of this. He was not used to dealing with feelings, not his own, not anyone else's. "So, what's up, Christo? You sound way too serious," he said flippantly.

"Yeah." Chris halted, unable for a moment to continue, to keep his voice from cracking. "It's about Reeni...and me."

"I figured that much," Aron said. "Reeni—you guys all right? I kinda wondered when you showed up this morning alone. I mean, Reeni's usually out here surfing with us. Don't' tell me you guys are breaking up, for god's sake!"

"No. No, it's nothing like that." Chris paused, before swearing under his breath, "Shit, I wish it were that simple. No. We're not about to break up. Actually we're about to have a baby. Reeni's—"

"Pregnant?" Aron rolled to his back and sat upright, staring at his friend. "You guys are pregnant—Jesus, Christo, how'd *that* happen?"

Chris laughed, but his laugh was hollow, empty of its usual humor. "Well, like my daddy told me a couple of years ago, *the first one can come at any time, after that it takes nine months.* He sure as shit was right about that!"

"Damn...Christo, you know what I mean. I mean, I figured you guys were probably doing it. I just figured that you be using some sort of...uh, *protection.* You know what I mean?"

"Well, it's like that—or, at least, it was like that. I mean, actually, for a long time we weren't going all the way. Close a couple of times, but then we'd stop. We kind of agreed to help each other stop before it was too late. Then, we didn't. Actually, it was right here…on this ledge." Chris paused, and as Ari opened his mouth, he waved him off saying, "Let me finish.

"Remember that hot weekend last month, just after those president holidays? Well, Reeni and I were surfing here late in the afternoon. You'd left, so had the other guys. We were alone. The surf had died down, and Reeni came in to the ledge to catch a few rays, to dry off in the sun."

Chris paused momentarily to watch as Alfredo began paddling toward shore. "I stayed out, just kind of dicking around, waiting for one last wave. When I finally gave up and came in, Reeni was lying here on a towel. I knelt down to kiss her, and she pulled me down, her bikini top was untied, it kinda slipped off, and, well, things just started happening…Pretty soon we were stripped down to nothing at all, and then…well, all thinking stopped, we were just doing…not thinking."

Chris paused. He looked over at Aron and smiled. "It was nice, Ari…and it was long. Not like those 'slam-bam-thank-you-ma'am' numbers that we've heard about down on the Pacific Street. We were taking our time and I guess…well, that's why we didn't think, but this time we'd gone too far, we'd just gone too far. You know what I'm trying to say?"

Aron nodded. But Chris could clearly see that Aron's attention was no longer with him. Aron was looking intently at the two surfers coming up the beach. Alfredo, a tall, dark-haired youngster whose black hair curled naturally around his face and who looked much younger than his eighteen years, was in the lead, carrying his board under his arm. His looks, however, belied his stature, for he stood about six feet and broad-shouldered. Mario followed, his board balanced neatly atop his head. He had the makings of being as tall and broad as his older brother, but for now he was the typically skinny kid who hadn't yet begun to fill out.

As the two brothers came toward the ledge, both smiling broadly, Alfredo, shouting a hello, called them both by name. Chris waved a greeting to them both. Aron did not. Rising to his knees, his arms folded tightly around his chest, he waited until both surfers were abreast the ledge and some three feet below them. Chris had stood now and was quietly stepping to the side. Knowing well what was about to happen, knowing Aron's inability to control his temper, he wanted no part in the conversation.

Aron, keeping his voice neutral, said, "Just what are you guys up to?"

Alfredo's smile that had been a natural partner with the warmth of his greeting faded quickly. "What do you mean—we're surfing…that's what we're *up to*. Is there a problem here?" His words were deliberately clipped and brittle.

"You damn betcha there's a problem here. You're the problem. You don't belong here," Aron continued. "This is our beach—and we don't allow your kind here. We don't want our water polluted."

"Polluted??? What the hell—"

"Yeah, you heard me," Aron interrupted. "Polluted." Chris reached over and laid his hand on Aron's wrist. "Come on Ari...relax a little. These are good guys—"

"Screw that noise, Christo," Aron barked, shaking his wrist free of Chris' grasp. "We don't want *spics* on our beach. It's just that simple. You guys," he continued to Alfred and Mario "just take one last hike to your car and stay off from our turf. This is our beach. *Wetbacks* have no place at Los Lobos."

Chris, shaking his head, looked over at the two. He could see that Alfredo was ready to take Ari on—and Chris himself, as well, if it came down to it. "Hey, Alfredo, why don't you guys take off for now. We can take care of this later. No point in duking it out right here. At least, that looks to be the next thing on the agenda."

"Yeah, Chris, you're probably right," Afredo said, looking squarely at Aron. But don't think I'm backing down. *Spic...wetback...*that's pretty ugly language in this day and age. Tell me, Chris, just where the fuck is your *buddy* coming from?"

Without waiting for an answer, Alfredo hefted his board and nodding to Mario, made off to the cliffside path that led to the Los Lobos Road, calling back to the two on the ledge, "*Hasta luego.*"

"Shit!" Aron turned to Chris, his face contorted with anger. He was not as tall as his friend, but his stocky frame was taut from the confrontation. "We'll get them, Christo. I promise. They'll never even *think* of surfing Los Lobos again."

Meanwhile, Mario, trudging along behind Alfredo, wanted to speak, but understood that there wasn't much that his older brother wanted to hear from him. Finally, because of Alfredo's silence and the anger that was visibly growing in the hunch of his bare shoulders and in the lock-step of his stride, Mario spoke. "You know, Fredo, we're not what he said. We're not *wetbacks*. The *guy* doesn't know from shit. You can't let that dumb-shit's dumb-shit comments get to you."

Alfredo stopped suddenly even as Mario quit speaking. Spinning around to confront his little brother, he stared down into Mario's upturned face. Several seconds passed before Alfredo dropped his board on the sage alongside the path. Two long steps and he was chest-to-shoulder in front of his little brother. He reached down and grasped Mario's chin, pulling his face close.

"No, Littlebrother. We're not *wetbacks*," he spat the last word out between clenched teeth. "And we're not *spics*. And that *pueto*'s going to learn that in spades. We may be living in the Village now. But my roots—your roots—are with *our* people downtown. And don't you ever forget it. Now let's get to the 'stang."

III

Monday noon. The school day was almost half over. Lunch break for the juniors and seniors had started. The freshmen and sophomores were heading to their fifth period classes, prior to their own lunch hour. Mario, small for his age, but showing signs via his big hands and size eleven shoes, was walking with Bobby Wilkens, a new-found surfing buddy, and Billy Jacobson to his English class. Their conversation was animated for they had just begun reading *Of Mice and Men* and were laughing good-naturedly about George's problems with Lennie. Thus, Mario, when he was blind-sided by Aron's clubbing punch to the temple, did not even see his attacker at first. He felt the pain of the blow and slipped to his knees, dropping his backpack. His two friends saw Aron, but did not see the blow. Aron simply looked at the young man on his knees, bleeding from his ear, called him *Spic*, and walked on.

Chris was walking with Reeni a few paces behind Aron and saw with alarm the entire incident. He stopped and stooped to grasp the youngster from behind at the armpits to help him up.

"Hey, kid," Chris said to Mario. "What's going on here? How'd you come to deserve that?"

Mario, fighting back the tears that began forming, simply shook his head. Billy picked up Mario's backpack; Bobby took out his handkerchief to press against Mario's head, saying to Chris, "Didja hear what he called Mario? What's he trying to do?"

The small crowd of students that had begun to gather about Mario was pressing for a fight...and Chris knew that if Alfredo showed up right now, there *would* be a fight, a big one. He took Mario by one arm while Reeni collected the backpack from Billy. Together they walked him to the restroom where Chris eased Mario through the door. He walked him to the basin, and, saturating the handkerchief with cool water, made a compress to staunch Mario's bleeding temple.

"We've gotta work this problem out, you know," Chris told him as he washed the split over Mario's ear that had caused all the blood. "I'll get to Ari, but meanwhile, you gotta put this behind you, whatever happened here. I'll help you. I'll work on Ari. He's just hotheaded. He didn't mean anything..."

Mario yanked Chris's hand away from his head. "Did you hear him? Did you hear what he said? He called me *spic*—just like he did me and Alfredo yesterday at Los Lobos. You're saying he didn't mean anything?" Mario had begun crying—from anger, from hurt, from frustration. "He's a fucking asshole…he thinks he can get away with anything."

"Hey, Mario. Come on! We can handle this. We got to work *together*. You hear me? I'm on your side on this one, buddy!"

Mario began to squirm under Chris's grasp. "Hold on a minute, kid," Chris said. "Just let me just finish wiping you up."

Chris was rinsing the handkerchief when suddenly the door to the restroom banged open. Alfredo stood there staring at the bloodied handkerchief, at Mario's tear-strained face, at Chris. "What the hell you doing to my little brother, you shit! Get away from him!"

"Wait, Fredo," Mario backed away from Chris. "It's okay, Fr—"

"It's not *okay*, Littlebrother. Nothing's okay *at all*. He's with them. Don't let him mess with your head. He's with that *hibrido*, they're in this together, and that *hibrido*'s gonna pay for this! Let me see your head."

"Alfredo!" Chris interrupted, dropping the wet handkerchief into the basin. "You gotta listen to me! I know it's not okay. Listen! I know it's not okay," he repeated, "but –"

Alfredo, pushing him aside, waved his hand in Chris's face. "Forget you!" He reached over to cradle Mario's head in his cupped hands. "Just get the hell outta here," he muttered. "I'll take over. Mario's my brother. I can handle it. Just get lost!"

IV

Lunchtime at Mission High School for many of the seniors meant lunch at the *Villager*, a Mom-and-Pop food stop that wasn't Mom-and-Pop at all from 11:30 to 1:00 weekdays. It was *the* hangout, the place to pick up sandwiches and the ubiquitous fries and cokes. Chris pulled into the parking lot of the complex, knowing that, as late as he was, there'd be few parking places near the *Villager* and that he and Reeni would have to get their sandwiches to go. He also recognized that he'd be confronting Ari. And he was right, for there sitting at one of the outdoor cement picnic tables was Aron, laughing and talking with a group of their friends, including Geoff and Buddy.

Reeni, taking Chris's arm, pulled him toward the take-out window, saying quietly, "Just let it pass for now, Chris. Please. Let's not have a scene here. It can wait."

"Well...Maybe. Yeah, you're right. Let's order, first, okay?" Chris replied. "We're already late, and I don't need another tardy for sixth period."

They ordered – the usual. Chris, his tri-tip sandwich and fries, a coke; Reeni, her chicken salad—no fries, ice tea. Ari, noticing the two of them at the window, called to them. Chris turned to stare at his best friend. Pausing momentarily, he walked over to Aron and, standing above him, said purposely loud enough for all to hear, "That was a chicken-shit trick you pulled, Ari. I thought we were pretty good friends. I don't know what's got into you."

Aron, starting to stand up, fell back into his seat as Chris pushed him violently back down. "You're way outta line, pal," Aron muttered. "You don't know what you're talking about."

"No, Ari," Chris retorted. "*You're* out of line. You had no call to smack that kid. He wasn't doing nothing to you."

"He's a *sp—*" Aron tried to speak, but Chris jabbed at him forcefully on the side of his mouth. "Don't even say it. Don't ever say it again," Chris replied between clenched teeth, his dark eyes flashing. "You're fixing to start something that not you, not anyone of us, is going to be able to handle. You don't know it yet, but you're about to get in way over your head."

Aron, rubbing his cheek gingerly, looked up at Chris. "Well, I guess I was wrong about one thing, Christo...I though you were my friend." Aron looked back at his friends sitting at the table, saying, "See ya, buddy."

"Yeah, well," Chris replied backing away and turning to pay for the sandwiches, "I *am* your friend – or at least,

I'm trying to be, Ari. You just don't seem to understand the problems that you're unleashing here—On all of us."

"That right?" Aron, now standing, shot back. "Well, you, pal, can just go fuck yourself! I don't need no *barrio* buddy!"

Chris picked up his order, and taking Reeni's hand, merely looked at Aron and shook his head.

V

Mario, seated in Mission High School's Discipline Center, was waiting for his meeting with the disciplinarian. He hadn't been prepared for the call and had no idea who had reported to the office what he was certain was the thing with Ari. He'd gotten to English class late, but was in his seat for only a few minutes when the call slip arrived. Seated in the Discipline Center now, he had only a vague idea of what was about to happen. He'd never been in trouble at school before, never been in any of the kinds of trouble that would bring him to a seat in the Discipline Office. And he was acutely aware that he sat there with his jacket zipped up almost to his chin. Alfredo had insisted that he take off his blood-stained tee-shirt and wear his jacket until Alfredo's lunchtime when his older brother would take him home to get another shirt.

Thus, when the call actually came, the disciplinarian, Mr. Beck, seemed initially friendly, relaxed. He made Mario feel somewhat less tense, asking if he was Mario Miguel Alhambra and confirming that he was relatively new to Mission High. He also asked him about the swelling that had been budding around the gash above his right ear. Mr. Beck even got up from his chair to inspect the wound more closely, commenting that the bloody wound looked pretty fresh.

"That's a pretty nasty bump you got yourself there, Mario. Want to tell me about it?" he remarked as he inspected the gash.

"Well," Mario stumbled. "It's really not much. Just an accident with the door to the bathroom." It was an excuse he had concocted only moments earlier, while sitting in the office.

"Hmmm. That's not exactly the story that I hear," Mr. Beck replied. "Actually, I pretty much know the story, Mario. And, while I guess you might not want it known around Mission High that you ratted on your fellow student…Well, actually, in this case, we are beyond that."

Mr. Beck, returning to his seat behind the desk, looked over at Mario with both concern and patience. "I'll tell you what. How about you unzip your jacket for me. I want to see your tee-shirt. I hear that it's pretty bloody."

"I can't unzip it, Mr. Beck. I don't have no shirt on."

"So where is it? Did you trash it?" Mr. Beck questioned.

"No! I'd never do something that stupid!" Mario looked up defiantly. He knew that he had been put into the tight corner, the very one he had he imagined as he sat waiting for this interview. He had no answers, but truthful ones. And he fidgeted in his seat as he realized where this conversation was leading.

Mr. Beck leaned back in his chair, fingering the file folder in which he had stored the background information on Mario and today's incident. "Okay. Mario. Let's just get down to the facts here. First, you got sucker-punched—at least that was the term I heard—by a senior, Aron Levin. Right on or over the left ear. I can see that from here! Next, Chris Battleson gets you into the restroom to clean you up. Your brother Alfredo comes in. Finishes the job. And bingo! you're off to English class. Did I miss anything?"

"Yeah, you did, sir. You missed something that's pretty important," Mario whispered, staring down at his shoes. "As long as you know that much you should know something else. You missed that that guy called me a *spic*." Mario looked up rebelliously, but the tears were beginning to form again. "He had no right to call me that!"

Beck tried, and knew he failed, to keep from registering his shock at hearing Mario's admission. "Yeah, you're right," he responded slowly. "Absolutely no right at all. And, we'll deal with that *this afternoon*, trust me. Meanwhile, what am I gonna do with you. You want to stay here the rest of the day? Or do you want to go home? It's just about your lunch time."

"Well, Mr. Beck, I have to go home to get another shirt. Fredo told me to. He's even going to miss his sixth period class to drive me. You probably shouldn't know that, but it seems that you know everything else, you might as well know that too." Mario smiled weakly for the first time since the lively discussion with his classmates about

George's problem with Lennie had been so utterly interrupted.

It was an engaging smile, and Mr. Beck laughed. "Not a problem, son. We can get Alfredo out of class for this kind of *emergency!*" He stood up motioning Mario to the door. "You just get yourself a clean shirt and be back for seventh period. Okay? And, Mario, you're somewhat new here at Mission. But, understand: we don't cotton to the language that Aron Levin used...Not here, not at any time!"

Mario, nodding, left the office, but heard Mr. Beck asking his secretary to get "Aron Levin, 12th grade, into this office, pronto!" Mr. Beck disappeared back into his office after having extracted Aron Levin file from the cabinet.

When Aron appeared in the Discipline Center some minutes later, he was immediately ushered into Beck's office. It was a short meeting. Mr. Beck, having greeted him at the door with a terse "Come in, please, Mr. Levin," reviewed the facts of the episode and questioned Aron about his role in the "sucker-punching" incident. Aron visibly flinched when he heard the descriptive phrase, but did not deny hitting Mario. When Beck accused him of using a racial epithet, Aron sat up in the chair.

"No way, sir. I wouldn't use that kind of language. That's just not my style!" Aron insisted.

Mr. Beck quietly opened the file on his desk and pulled a sheet of paper, describing it as a short list of names of students who had overheard his remark. "You still denying you called that young man a *"spic?"*

Aron lowered his head to stare at his clenched fists which were clasped tightly across his chest. "No, I guess not..." he muttered. "But I didn't sucker-punch him. I just tapped him on the cheek!"

Mr. Beck stared momentarily across the desk at the young man sitting before him. And then, as Aron sat there listening, he dialed up his Aron's father and described the incident, relating to him the disposition of this problem. "Aron," Beck affirmed, "will be suspended for three school days and will be serving eight-hour detentions on the following four Saturdays after his return to Mission."

Mr. Beck tapped the pencil he was holding on his desk, waiting, listening, then answered, "Yes, Mr. Levin. We do have several witnesses—students who have both identified Aron and corroborated the exact words he used."

Again there was a pause before Mr. Beck again replied. "Yes, Mr. Levin. Aron's will be an in-school suspension. We want the suspended to be students here on the campus and at task—"

Tapping his pencil, Mr. Beck listened for a moment before responding, "His studies? Well, we regularly ask a student's teachers—in this case, Aron's—to supply work, including tests, to the detention supervisor. It's...excuse me, Mr. Levin, please let me finish. It is up to the individual teachers—whether they allow suspended students to complete assignments. Some teachers do, others don't. It is the individual classroom teacher's prerogative."

Again, Mr. Beck paused, listening, before replying. "Well, that is a problem that you will have to resolve with Aron's teachers. How his teachers choose to handle Aron's suspension is out of my hands. It is *their* classroom, *their* decision. Please understand that I do appreciate your concern. However, on the face of it, Mr. Levin, it is Aron's actions and language that have provoked this problem. Maybe, your son must face up to his responsibility for this matter. Meanwhile, I do thank you for your hearing me out and I apologize for bringing you this distressing news."

Returning the receiver to the phone's cradle, Mr. Beck turned to Aron. "Well, Mr. Levin, you've heard the news. Maybe you will understand that here at Mission High School we simply don't tolerate that kind of language...And it *is* the language issue—the sucker-punch was nasty—the language is intolerable and ugly."

As Aron left the office, the smirk on his face belied the turmoil that was causing his stomach to churn. "Three days! And four Saturdays! Well, this is *not* the end of this little game," Aron muttered as he slammed the outside door to the Discipline Center.

VI

Monday afternoon, still troubled by his encounter with both Alfredo and Mario and his growing depression with Ari and his attitude problems, Chris Battleson took the steps to the rectory at Saint Monica's Catholic Church two at a time. Not that he was in a hurry: he was just enormously nervous. Ringing the doorbell, he literally hopped from one foot to another, and old Mrs. Bell, opening the door on this scene, accepted Chris's hyperactivity as symptomatic of his *persona*. She'd been the housekeeper for the pastor, Father Leo Meagher, for the past twenty years and had known Chris for many of these years. Nor did she think it odd that Chris should show up unannounced. Chris had always been a frequent drop-in, one of the few in St. Monica's parish afforded that luxury. Fr. Leo truly liked—and even had grown to respect—this young man.

Mrs. Bell, asking Chris to wait in the entry hall, intercommed Fr. Leo, telling him about his unexpected visitor. And Chris heard the priest's welcoming laugh, telling her to "send young Mr. Battleson up."

Chris took the stairs to Fr. Leo's study two at a time as well, apparently still unable to contain himself even as he knocked at the open door. Fr. Leo looked up, smiling. "Well, Mr. Battleson...what brings you off the waves and the tennis courts? It's way too nice out there to be visiting an old man!"

"Yeah, well, Father Leo, I just thought I'd drop by. I was just kind of driving through the neighborhood..."

Father Leo, motioning for Chris to sit, smiled and looked down at his desk, reaching for his favorite *toy*: a spring-loaded hand exerciser. It was a game that he played whenever he surmised, as he had by the look on Chris's face, that what was coming was going to be more than just a drop-by visit. Much more.

Father Leo—Father Leonardo Meagher, Chicago-born, son of a Sicilian mother and an Irish-American father, had been down the road apiece. Now a sixty-year-old priest who'd been pastor at St. Monica's for the past twenty-two years, he felt comfortable both with his life in the parish and his understanding of the varied worlds of his parishioners, a parish that was growing increasingly a melting pot of California's ethnic varieties.

"Maybe, we'd better skip the formalities," he said, flexing the exerciser and smiling up at Chris.

Chris, looking up from his hands, knew well the twinkling smile and saw through his mentor's ploy. Yes, Father Leo saw through Chris's failed attempt at nonchalance. Yes, he noted silently Chris's tightly clasped hands. Yes, he was quietly waiting for Chris to begin.

Chris had known Father Leo since he began first grade at St. Monica's Elementary School. He had been, and still was on special occasions, a parish altar boy. He'd had summer jobs at the parish for years during his early teens. And, Father Leo had always been the first to know of Chris's youthful traumas, and Chris had relied upon him to come through—if not always with solutions, certainly always with the time to listen and, of course, with the reassuring smile.

Indeed, Father Leo knew well the traumas of youth. As the second son of an intensely Catholic (Irish and Italian...could it be other wise?) household, Leonardo had been raised to the priesthood. He'd entered the seminary out of high school, for that was what had been expected of him. He'd completed his studies and been ordained, only to begin to question his commitment to the priesthood when he was first assigned as a newly-ordained priest to an affluent parish in a suburb near Lake Forest. It was this assignment—as the "flunky" priest—that initiated the doubts: his parish work was with the very old—bingo games, bingo games, bingo games—and with the day-to-day supervision of the elementary school, all tasks that the pastor and the other two assistants had had little time or inclination for. Father Leo spent the better part of a hesitant year there before applying for and being granted permission to join the military as a chaplain. It was 1966 and was the *career* move that changed everything.

Doubts disappeared as he moved with platoon after platoon in the swamps of Viet Nam. He learned things…language…hopes and dreams…failures… fears… of young men his own age. And he grew in wisdom as he talked things through with such men as what he came to believe were his parish. He'd "re-enlisted" because, over time, his goals as a priest came to be realized in the souls of these troubled men, men who were never simply "Catholic" or "protestant" or "Jewish."

His Viet Nam years became the defining moments of his early ministry. His ability to listen, to counsel, to reassure were securely embedded during these years in the jungles and swamps of war-torn villages. He learned that he, too, could admit to fear and failure, to hopes and dreams, and not be less than the priest he imagined he was, the priest he knew he could be. He also learned that the teachings that were supposed to anchor his calling did not always supply answers to the evils that one faces in this anguish-prone world that he had come to know intimately.

Thus, he could subtly joke this afternoon with Chris. He could wait patiently for the opening that Chris would give him.

And Chris did. "Father," he began, "I gotta problem. And…and, I need to…I need help."

Father Leo, quietly flexing his hand exerciser, heard the serious tone that Chris had suddenly taken on and looked over at the youngster: yes, he knew well Chris' growing maturity, yet he still thought of Chris as a kid. "Let's see what we can do," he said. "Maybe if we talk it out, it won't seem quite so serious…or as overwhelming as your tone suggests. You want to just lay it out for both of us?"

"Well," Chris began, "you know Reeni and I are pretty

serious? We're thinking about getting married—not right now! but soon, maybe as soon as I can get my schooling and EMT licensing finished and get a job."

"Yes...I think I figured out what I didn't actually know for sure," Father Leo grinned. "You two have been pretty obvious about your feelings for each other. What's the matter...she about to dump you?"

"No...no. That's not the problem. The problem is Reeni. She's uh...preg—gonna have a baby." Chris had dropped his eyes. He was staring intently at his fists tightly clenched in his lap. He knew that Father Leo would be disheartened by the news, disappointed in him. And he hated facing his old friend. He was fearful, now that the words were out, lying there on the desk between them, that the priest would ask for details – like "How could you let this happen." He knew that such a question would be his mother's first response. And he didn't have—couldn't explain, as he had tried to with Ari – such answers.

Father Leo, however, saw the approaching trap and was well practiced in dodging the obvious. He had, in his time, talked with too many GIs to ask the stupid questions. "So what's the plan here, Christopher?" he began. Then, realizing that Chris was not yet up to dealing with the future, he quickly amended himself. "How about if I ask some questions...you answer as best you can...if you can't, I'll understand. But let's, right now, just see some things clearly. First off, have you talked with your Mom and Dad? With Reeni's parents?"

Chris continued looking down at the fists clenched in his lap. "No. Neither of us has. I guess—no, I know, we're both scared to. They're gonna be mad—and, well, pissed—if you'll pardon me, Father."

Father Leo laughed quietly. "Christopher—this is no time for a language lesson. I've heard the word before, trust me. And I suspect I'll hear it again…in this very office. So, let's just go on."

He paused and then got up from his desk and went around to the front of it to stand just in front of Chris. "Hey, Christopher. How about looking up at me? I can take it! And if you don't relax those knuckles, you're going to break them. So let's just ease up a little. You're making *me* tense!" Chris looked up, smiling feebly. "Okay, Father. I'm sorry. I just don't know what to do. I don't think that I've ever felt so confused."

"No. I suspect that you're correct—you haven't. Which, I also suspect, is why we're sitting here. Right?"

Chris smiled again and nodded.

Father Leo nodded as well and continued, "How about another question? What does Reeni think about all of this? I mean, what is she saying?"

"Reeni? She's about as miserable as I am. I mean, we still love each other…It's just that we both feel that we have let down—disappointed—everyone. We both don't know what to do next."

"Okay," Father Leo leaned back against the desk, his hands resting on the edges. "How far along is she? I mean, when did—no, when is the baby due—do you know? And has she been to the clinic?"

"Uh, well, the baby's about a month along. Yeah, she just came back from the doctor's there last Friday. So, we're sure. Anyway, it was just about a month ago. If that's what you're asking…"

'Well, yes, I guess that is what I was asking. Okay, let's

get down to some specifics. As I see it, you both have three options to consider." He continued after pausing to look at Chris. "First," he said, "you could get an abortion. Second, you could have the baby and put it up for adoption. And third, you could have the baby and raise it as your own—which, of course, it is."

Chris staring up at his priest, nodded dully, absently wiping at the tears that were forming at the corners of his eyes. Father Leo quietly moved back to his desk, and reached into the bottom drawer for a tissue which he passed across the desk to Chris. The priest turned away from Chris to face the window.

"Chris," he said gently, "before we go any further, you have to know that tears are not a new thing around here. You certainly aren't the first, and you won't be the last. And, just so you know where I'm coming from, the first time I saw a young man cry was in Viet Nam. And he wasn't the only one in that distressed country either. Sometimes tears are as much a sign of frustration as of anything else. Frustration is a pretty intense emotion for even the strongest of men."

"Thanks, Father. I guess I just didn't know it was coming. And yes, I'm frustrated—and scared. Reeni's frustrated and frightened, as well. We both feel that everything is suddenly out of control. We don't know where we are going from here," Chris whispered, looking up at the back of the priest and wiping the tears away.

Father Leo, still staring out the window, folded his arms across his chest, saying, "Christopher, let's get back to the options. Those three seem to be a starting—Oh, my! Christopher, come here. Quickly!"

Chris took the few steps beyond Father Leo's desk to stare out the window following the priest's pointing finger. They both watched, Chris in shock, as Reeni crossed the street and approached the front door of the rectory. She was a typical high school senior, strong of character, a fierce competitor, an energetic captain of Mission's varsity volleyball and soccer teams, an avid surfer.

Reeni simply exuded energy. And she was charming. Her charisma began with her smile, a smile that lighted up her entire frame. Not one's usually willowy teen, Reeni was sturdy to the point of being muscular—a fact that she absolutely abhorred, but knew that she couldn't do much about if she continued her active sports' life. And continuing that life-style was far more important to her that what others might think of her figure. So she dressed carefully and well, favoring pastel colors, which enhanced her tanned skin, and chose tailored skirts and blouses. Coming up the walk, her stride was her typical purposeful pace—light, firm, focused.

"Father, Reeni! She can't come up here. She can't see me crying. I've got to get out of here," Chris cried as he bolted toward the door.

"Christopher. No! You get back here and sit down. You forget, I'm still in charge of this place." Father Leo moved to his intercom phone, calling "Mrs. Bell?"

Chris heard her immediate reply and listened as the priest told her to ask Reeni to wait in the lower office...that Father Leo would be "with her soon." Slumping in his chair, Chris looked up at the priest, the same feeble smile parting his lips. "Okay, Father. I'm sorry. I guess nothing I do right now has much to do with thinking. I want to see Reeni. But I'm really…I dunno…just feeling so sad, I guess."

"Okay, but Christopher, give me a break. I know a little bit about what's going through your thick skull…And, you probably are, more than a little sad. You should be. You got some really heavy moments ahead of you." Smiling softly, Father Leo had moved back to lean on the front edge of his desk, his hand resting lightly on Chris' shoulder. "Okay. Now, Chris, what do you say to pulling yourself together while I go down and see Reeni. Can I tell her that you're here and up in my office? Can I bring her up?"

Chris smiled openly for the first time. "Yeah. That'd be a good idea. Maybe if we both talk with you, together, I mean, maybe together we can begin to make some sense of this mess."

It was a mere matter of minutes before Chris heard Father Leo on the stair, talking with Reeni, as he approached the upper office. Chris stood and, as Reeni entered the room ahead of the priest, approached and embraced her. Father Leo pulled another chair to the side of Chris's and beckoned both of the youngsters to sit. They did so, but Chris held tightly onto Reeni's hand.

"Well, now," the priest began as he sat down behind his desk. "Let's all make sure that we understand where we might want to go from here. Chris has pretty much filled me in on the problem here, Reeni…I've told him of the options, as I see them. Let me run through them for you." And Father Leo, this time using his fingers for emphasis, outlined the three propositions. Reeni, hearing the first option, abortion, vehemently shook her head; however, Father Leo motioned for Reeni to let him continue. Hearing the other two options, Reeni slowly nodded her head in comprehension. And as with Chris a few moments earlier, she began quietly to cry. And Father Leo for a second time got up from his desk and reached into the bottom drawer to hand her a tissue.

He sat back down behind his desk, picked up his *toy*, and stared down at his closed hand for a moment. A moment which turned into several minutes. He listened to the clock ticking quietly across the room before he began. "Well," he finally said, "We *do* have some starting places." He looked up at Chris and Reeni and waited until they, too, looked over at him. "First," he continued, "know that some of this is going to sound downright *trite*. But it isn't. Not by any means. I think a lot of the time just plain old common sense comes out sounding trite, but it *is still* common sense. You follow me?"

Chris and Reeni both nodded their heads, but neither attempted to speak.

"Good, so let's get at it, shall we?" Father Leo again stood up and walked back to the window. "Okay, here's number one: it's not by any means the end of the world. You two are in company with a long — historically long — line of good people. Doesn't much help the pain or the sadness or the frustration. But there it is…"

He turned to the pair of youngsters. "So, it's not the end of the world…in fact, if you want to look at it…it's the beginning of a new life. And you two lovely people are its creators. You just might consider yourselves awesome — perhaps not right now, but down the road not very far."

Still smiling softly, he looked over at the two who were still holding hands…but whose tension was lessening. He decided to continue. "Here's what I think I can do to help. But remember, this is your moment, as it were, so you have to be square with me. If I say something that doesn't sell with either one of you...well, you have to be honest. That a deal?"

Both Reeni and Chris nodded their heads, Chris began smiling, and Father Leo was relieved to see that there was little of the earlier strained tension about his mouth. "Okay, so first things first...I gather from Chris that neither of you has told your parents about this...uh, .situation. Right?"

Watching them both nod their heads, Reeni quite vigorously, even as the tears began at the corners of her eyes again, Father Leo moved to the front of his desk to rest against it and to be close to both Reeni and Chris. "Fine," he said. "Here's what. Why don't I just call them both to meet with me tomorrow night. That's Tuesday. They don't have to know right off that I have invited both parents. We can cross that bridge when they arrive. They'll know soon enough anyway!" And he laughed gently at the thought. "Next, I will want you two here as well—I don't want them to think that I'm playing games with anyone of you. And anyway, you're both going to have to face them sooner or later. It might as well be here where—"

Chris held up his hand as if to halt Father Leo, half interrupting the old priest. "No, Father, I can't let you do that! I mean, I—we—really appreciate what you are saying, but it's not fair to put you on the spot like that."

"Whoa! I know what you mean, Chris, but, trust me, I'm not putting myself in any position that I don't think is wise—or that I don't feel comfortable with. Just hear me out, okay?"

Chris nodded his head, and Reeni reached across and touched him on the cheek, as if to say, *It's all right.*

"So. Here's the deal. You guys be here about seven-thirty or so tomorrow evening. I'll set up the meeting with your parents for eight. For all they know, it's about Parish Council business. Both your dads, as you know, are pretty active in council business here at St. Monica's, so it's going to seem natural."

Father Leo reached over and took Chris by the forearm, indicating that the meeting was about over. He wanted them to know that their problem was his problem and that resolutions were in the offing. Chris stood, pulling Reeni up with him. Father Leo reached over with his left hand and took Reeni's in his own. "Just remember—you two are good people. Your future child is in most blessed hands! But, remember too: tomorrow night is not going to be a cake walk! Your parents love you dearly and have their own visions of your future. And I'm pretty sure that this particular vision is not among theirs!"

Shepherding the two toward the door of his office, he continued, "But remember this as well: You both have your own innate goodness on our side. And we have the love of Jesus on our side. So, just go in peace and be happy for each other."

VII

Alfredo had done as he promised: he'd taken Mario home to get a clean shirt. And on the drive, Mario had spilled all of the afternoon's proceedings across the interior of the Alfredo's Mustang—including an exact reproduction of his meeting with Mr. Beck. And he concluded by relating to his older brother the last words that he heard the Disciplinarian say to his secretary as Mario left the office. "I think the prick's in for it big time, Fredo," he finished. "The old man seemed really pissed."

And, Alfredo had been called, as he had expected, into Mr. Beck's office upon his return at seventh period. And it was no call slip; the call came over the school's intercom for the entire school population to hear. Mr. Beck smiled to himself as he heard the announcement. *That'll give that arrogant young man, Mr. Levin, something to chew on,* he thought to himself.

Alfredo's meeting with the disciplinarian had been short, a kind of "Yes-sir, those-are-the-facts-sir" meeting. And now, at work, Alfredo was thinking over the events of the past two days. "Aron Levin and his in-your-face-attitude would not simply disappear," Alfredo mused aloud as he knelt on the floor and restocked the hair products' shelves at the Village Pharmacy. He would start the deliveries in about an hour; meanwhile, his workload was usually whatever was needed. Today, it was restocking shelves. He had begun training to handle the pharmacy's medical counter — a job he really looked forward to: more pay, more chance to interact with people, less boring than shelving and delivering. *Aron Levin...what a turd!* Alfredo reflected. *He can't keep this up. This shit's gotta stop. I don't want to find myself in the middle of a street battle. But, Jesus! Attacking Mario. Damn! That's really low. The freaking cretin!*

Alfredo was so engrossed in his thinking that he didn't even see Carlos until Carlos tapped him on the top of his head. "Hey, honcho, you must really be into stocking shelves! I even said 'hello' and you didn't look up!" Carlos Alvarez was Alfredo's cousin...sometimes big brother...always friend. A dark-skinned, broad-shouldered Mexican, his hair slicked back into a neat pony tail, he carried more than a hint of Indian in his strong face; he exuded a kind of muscle that created in those who didn't know him for his gentle side an apprehension, a fear that he was capable of doing much harm to those who pushed him even a little too hard. Few knew that his muscle came from hard work, work running the cattle ranch that had been in his family for generations. At twenty-three, he was very good at handling the ranch, the cattle that populated it, and the men who worked for him.

Carlos seldom smiled, but when he did—as he invariably did when he encountered Alfredo—his imposing stature melted before his good-natured, grinning countenance. The menace that one saw in his granite-like exterior was merely his façade: he'd been raised to expect trouble in his world, and he was determined to mask his gentler side with a face that he knew well could inspire others to bend to his will.

Alfredo looked up into the smiling countenance. "Hey, Carlitos…What's happening, man? No, I was just busy thinking bad thoughts!"

"Shit…Fredo…that means you're headed for the Confessional come Saturday. Bad thoughts mean sin big-time, dude!" Carlos was laughing even as he slapped Alfredo lightly on each cheek. Alfredo stood as Carlos backed up to give him room.

"No, not *those* kind of bad thoughts!" Alfredo, who matched his cousin's height, though not his breadth, laughed and tapped Carlos on the chin with his fist. "A different kind of bad thought actually. But, it's a real problem, Carlitos. Maybe, we should talk…You got some time on your hands?"

"For you, Fredo, I got all afternoon," Carlos responded. "Where can we talk?"

"Just give me minute to tell the old man that I'm taking a break, and we can go for a coke."

Within moments, Carlos and Alfredo were sitting across from one another at one of the cement, outdoor tables at the *Villager* across the parking lot from the *Village Pharmacy*. He described to Carlos the incidents, beginning with the episode at Los Lobos the day before and concluding with Aron's attack on Mario this afternoon. "So that's it, Carlitos. I guess the only good news is that the school is on our side," He finished up, "but, it's not over. This prick, Aron Levin, he ain't gonna quit. I can't believe he'd take out a freshman in front of the whole school! He's got balls."

Carlos sat, his chin resting on his cupped hands, staring back at his friend. "Not good, Honcho. Who's this Chris guy and what's his story?"

"Well, I think – I *think* – he's okay. He basically stood up for us yesterday on the beach. And he was helping Littlebrother in the bathroom when I got there. He might be pissed at me though...I wasn't too cool with him."

"Well, I say, screw *him*! And I got an idea...Let's us push some buttons, okay?"

Alfredo looked out onto the street, watching the cars pass by. "I don't know, Carlitos...I don't want big trouble. What you got in mind? "

"Well—" Carlos began, but was interrupted by Alfredo, waving his hand in front of him, and saying "Before you go on...you gotta know...I *want* to push some buttons real bad. They, well, this guy, Levin, he, can't do what he did to Littlebrother. It's just wrong. But it's scary too."

"Okay," Carlos said, laying his hand across Chris' forearm. "Let me have a say now! Let me find out who this Levin guy is. I can do this. And quickly too. Just gimme a day or two. I figure that we can put a little itch in him to quiet down. We can put some people on the street to give him a wakeup call. Just give me some time."

Carlos stood and pulled Alfredo up by the arm. "You

get back to the pharmacy. I got some work to do!" He smiled and Alfredo smiled at his buddy, his cousin, his friend. They walked back to the drug store together, and Carlos asked as Alfredo started to enter the store, "Say, where is Mario this afternoon? I thought he was helping you in the store these days."

Alfredo responded with a laugh that he had told Mario to stay at home and nurse his bruises. He was spending the night at Bobby's—they were working on some kind of project for their science class.

Carlos turned, waving back at Alfredo. "See ya, honcho. Stay cool! And stay out of trouble!"

VIII

Tuesday morning brought with it the usual morning springtime overcast, low clouds, fog along the San Marcos River, mist, gloom. Alfredo had just arrived at the school parking lot and was crossing through the lines of late arriving cars waiting to find available parking, when he saw Bobby Welkins walking alone onto the campus.

"Hey, Bobby!" he called, smiling, "where's Mario?"

Bobby stopped, calling back to Alfredo as he waited for Alfredo to catch up. "I dunno. He never showed up — after surfing yesterday. I thought we were supposed to work on the science thing. But..."

Alfredo's smile disappeared as a look of anxiety crossed his face. "What're you saying, he never showed up? He was supposed to spend the night with you. He didn't come home. We thought he was with you – at your house."

Bobby, still nonchalant, smiled, "Gee. I dunno. We left him at the Lobos, he said he was gonna catch a couple more waves. I had to get home to do some collecting for my paper route. When he didn't show up, I figured that he just went on home—or something..." Bobby's voice trailed off as he read the concern in Alfredo's face.

Alfredo, apprehension stiffening his entire body, said as much to himself as to Bobby, "What's this 'or something'?" and turned back, half-running to his car.

Chris Battleson, just squeezing his dark blue Toyota truck into a space, saw Alfredo, read the concern in his face, and hollered out his window, "Hey, Alfredo! What's happening?" He flicked the radio off to better hear Alfredo's response.

"It's Mario! I don't know where he is...He's missing...or something. I gotta find him."

Chris could not mistake the fear in Alfredo's eyes or the tremor in his voice. Backing his Toyota out of the parking space, he said, "Get in. Let me help you look."

"No. It's okay. It's my problem!" Alfredo halted, searching the parking lot, looking for signs of Mario's arrival.

"No. Get in," Chris repeated. "*Get in*. We're wasting time. I'll drive, you can look."

Alfredo, acquiescing, opened the passenger door even as Chris was starting to pull away. Jumping in and slamming the car door, he looked over at Chris who was maneuvering around the last arriving cars. "Let's start with home," he said. "Maybe he's home in bed. Maybe I—we—just missed him this morning. Maybe he's still asleep—the little turd!"

"Yeah, that's a good a place as any." Moments later, Chris, looking over and reading the tension in his passenger's body, continued, "So, Alfredo, lighten up a bit. That's probably it. He's home asleep. Meanwhile, why don't you give me some directions. I don't know where you live."

Alfredo's smile was a tight line across his face. "Yeah, I hope so." He looked over at Chris, pausing before he continued, "Sunset Ranch...you know, that new development over the bluffs leading into town?" He continued to watch Chris' face for any reaction, any reaction that might suggest surprise, a question—like *what's a Mex doing living in such high class digs.'*

But if the thought crossed Chris's mind, it wasn't registered in his demeanor. He just swung the car out into traffic and headed toward the bluffs. And Alfredo momentarily smiled. Such a thought, he acknowledged to himself bleakly, wasn't one that he would have had two days ago,

And relieved that he had seen no such reaction in Chris's demeanor, he continued. "Mario was supposed to spend the night with Bobby Wilkens last night. Nobody thought any different. They apparently went surfing yesterday after school. I didn't know about that...I was at work. Bobby says that Mario stayed on at Los Lobos after Bobby left to—"

Chris, pulling into the Sunset Ranch development, interrupted Alfredo, saying, "Surfing? Mario was surfing? Alone? *Shit!*"

Alfredo looked over at him, fear once again clouding his eyes. "Yeah. He was with Bobby and a couple of other kids. But Bobby says Mario stayed on after the other guys left. The little shit shouldn't have stayed on alone." Alfredo paused, before pointing out, "It's the green and grey house up on your right."

Chris pulled up into the driveway, and Alfredo was already opening the door as the truck pulled to a stop. "Wait here," he called. "I'll be just a minute."

Indeed, a bare minute passed before Alfredo returned. Settling quickly into the passenger's seat, he looked over at Chris, his eyes telling all, his anxiety turning to fright. "I got to go to Los Lobos. That's where he was. Take me back to school, I'll get my car–"

"No way, dude," Chris interrupted, starting his engine and backing into the street. "We'll both go. Anyway, we're already halfway there. Going back'll just waste time."

They drove in silence, past the still quiet downtown streets, out onto the narrow two-lane Los Lobos Road, the Pacific coming into view among the stands of chaparral and native oaks as they passed over the small hills and into the sand dunes. The only signs of life were the cattle grazing quietly in the pastures and along the hillsides. The early morning clouds cast a dreary pall across the entire valley, but the gloom seemed to grow and was especially bleak over the empty beach. Waves from the receding tide were darkly grey beneath the whited foam that formed an indiscriminate spread across the water.

Chris pulled into the empty parking lot as Alfredo again jumped from the still moving truck. "Shit!" he cried out "That's Mario's bike parked over there!"

Chris, shutting off the engine, quickly joined Alfredo to scan the beach; then, both set off on a quick trot to the surf's edge. Alfredo, choking back the lump that had all but clogged his speech, said, "You go up the beach, I'll go down this way. We've got to find something here."

And they did. Chris, loping up the strand, had crossed a small dune, before spotting a dark form lying at the edge of the water. Approaching the form, he immediately recognized Mario's skinny frame. His surfboard was half buried in the sand just at the receding tide's edge. Chris turned to call out to Alfredo even as he ran toward the small figure. Waving his arms, he watched momentarily as Alfred, hearing his call, turned back and sprinted down the beach toward Chris.

Chris was kneeling beside the unconscious Mario when Alfredo reached them. Alfredo saw that Mario had been strapped to his surfboard. His hands and feet, wrapped around and bound beneath the board, were half-buried in the sand. The board's skeg was firmly planted into the wet sand. Last night's advancing tide had washed sand up, almost burying the bottom of the board. Mario, dressed in only his shorts, lay face up, motionless, on the board.

"Littlebrother..." Alfredo cried, tears forming, "Littlebrother..." He stood there immobile, staring down at the unconscious Mario.

"Gimme your shirt," Chris said, stripping off his own flannel shirt. "We got to get him warm." Chris bent low over Mario's inert body, pressing his cheek to Mario's mouth. "He's breathing...but it's awful faint!" He began to wrap his shirt across Mario's thin chest, massaging some warmth into the youngster's ashen-blue frame. "Jesus! He's so friggin' cold! We need help." He grabbed the shirt from Alfredo's hand, quickly wrapping it too across Mario's inert form.

Chris stood, even as Alfredo dropped to his knees alongside his brother. "There's a blanket in the back of my truck. I'm going to get it. You see what you can do to get him untied. I'm going to call 911." He watched momentarily as Alfredo began searching beneath the board for the bungee cords that had been laced around Mario's ankles and that pinned his feet awkwardly under his surfboard. Mario's hands likewise disappeared under the board with another set of tightly stretched cords.

Watching him slowly, carefully, and thus clumsily, trying to lift his brother, Chris slipped back to his knees across from Alfredo. "No!" he cried out. "We have to untie him. I'm going to lift the board, you just get the cords off him!" And in so instructing Alfredo, Chris tipped the board, and Mario slipped inches down the upturned board to the sand. They both heard him moan quietly.

"Shit! You're hurting him," cried Alfredo, reaching over to slap at Chris's hand.

"Just fucking untie him, Alfredo!" Chris nearly bawled out. "We got to get him untied – and warm!"

Alfredo paused, staring down into Mario's face. His right hand moved to caress his little brother's ashen cheek. He pushed back the cold, wet, sand-sodden hair that had washed across and was now plastered to his brow. "Okay. Just hold on, Littlebrother. We'll get you out of here. Just hold on." Alfredo, his body shaking, had begun crying quietly again.

And with Chris balancing the board on its side, Alfredo quickly unfastened the bungee cords from beneath Mario's surfboard. Mario slipped from the board onto the wet sand.

Chris jumped to his feet as Alfredo tried gently to bring Mario to his lap. "Yeah. That's right, Alfredo. Get him on your lap and press him to your chest. He's probably got hypothermia. We need to get him warm and breathing. I'm gonna call for help. You stay here. We shouldn't move him by ourselves!"

Chris sprinted across the sand toward his Toyota and the cell phone. Alfredo, nodding up at Chris's retreating figure, pulled the limp body of his younger brother to his lap, readjusting the two flannel shirts across Mario's back and shoulders. Still crying silently, Alfredo began slowly rocking his brother back and forth. He blew his own breath across his brother's face, forcing warm air on the youngster's forehead and cheeks. With his other hand, he gently brushed sand away from Mario's eyes and mouth.

Chris, at his truck, was trying desperately to convince the voice on the other end of the phone of the emergency. "No, I don't know for sure, but I think it's hypothermia. Please just get an ambulance here as soon as possible." He paused, then answered, Yeah, we're in the parking lot—Los Lobos beach…There's a Toyota truck—the only car in the lot. No. We're not gonna move him. Please. Just get them here!"

Hanging up, Chris wondered about the time. *How much time*, he wondered, *did they have. Mario's in sore need of help.* Chris remembered reading the *Surfer's Journal* about hypothermia—what happened to the victim, how to treat the problem. The trouble was, he knew, that he didn't really remember the specifics. Snatching a blanket from the back of his truck, he thought about the details of the article as he jogged back to Alfredo.

"They're on the way, Alfredo," he said as he knelt down beside the two. "How's he doing? Any change?" Chris dropped the woolen blanket to the sand beside the two brothers.

"No." Alfredo answered continuing to rock the still inert Mario. "He's just not moving. I feel so helpless. I'm not doing anything. I don't know what's happening." Alfredo looked up at Chris, his eyes beginning to tear over once more.

"Hey, Alfredo, we've got help on the way. You're doing just fine!" He paused to spread the blanket across Mario's back and around Alfredo's shoulders. "We just got to hang in and help Mario to hang in," Chris said. "The important thing is to get him warm. And not move him. I remember reading that the cold affects the heart and brain and moving him can trigger some sort of screw-up. So we just have to sit here and wait for help. It's on the way."

Moments later, they both looked up as the siren from the ambulance reached them. Chris got up and began sprinting back toward the parking lot. He wanted to be there when the EMTs arrived. Jogging up to his car, he hoped that the EMTs were two that he knew. He'd been on drive-alongs with a couple of them in the last few months in preparation for his college studies. *It'd be better,* he thought, *if I knew them.*

The ambulance pulled silently into the gravel parking lot and next to the Toyota, an EMT exiting from the passenger side even as the vehicle came to a stop. "Hey, Chris. I didn't expect to see you here!" the EMT said, recognizing Chris. "Okay, whatta we got here?"

"Hey, Ike. Dang! I'm glad it's you! It's a kid, his name's Mario. He's down on the sand. We didn't want to move him. I think it's hypothermia. But I don't really know shit! He's unconscious. His brother's with him. Alfredo."

The other EMT, pulling a stretcher from the back of the ambulance, followed the two of them on the run down the sand. Coming up to the two brothers sitting at the edge of the surf, the EMT, Ike, spoke quietly. "Okay, Alfredo, we're here. You let us take over. We're going to gently lift him off of you and onto the stretcher. Here. Let me have the blanket." Ike peeled the blanket from off of Alfredo's shoulders and from around Mario's back. Lifting Mario easily onto the stretcher, Ike carefully tucked the blanket across the boy, leaving one of his arms outside of the blanket. He gently lay the youngster's arm across his chest.

Meanwhile, the other EMT inserted a breathing tube into Mario's trachea, then snapped the plastic tubing to an oxygen tank which he attached to the stretcher. They then quickly lifted the stretcher and began the jog back up the sand to the ambulance. Slipping the stretcher into the back of the rescue vehicle, Ike turned to Alfredo and Chris. "You guys can follow us back to the hospital. We'll know more by the time we get to the emergency room. Meanwhile, on the way, we're gonna start him on an IV – saline fluid, really—and some atropine – that'll bring up his heart rate. The ER can take it from there!"

Alfredo, watching as the other EMT climbed into the back of the ambulance, held up his hand. "Wait. I can ride with him, can't I. When he wakes up, I want to be with him…" His words trailed off as Ike, moving around to the driver's side, said, "No, Alfredo. It'd be better if you just met us at the hospital. We're going to do everything we can to get him help just as quickly as possible. Meanwhile, you just follow us—and get yourselves some shirts!"

Not waiting for an answer, Ike stepped into the driver's seat and started the engine, revving up the siren. The ambulance swung around and headed out of the parking lot. Chris pulled two sweat shirts from a duffle bag stashed behind the driver's seat. One he tossed to Alfredo; the other he pulled quickly over his head, Alfredo doing likewise. Both young men climbed into the Toyota and took off in the direction of the retreating ambulance. Neither spoke. Alfredo, staring straight ahead, saw nothing. Chris tailed the emergency vehicle, noting absent-mindedly the sun's attempt, mostly unsuccessful, to break through the morning overcast. Indeed, the gloom seem to have perceptibly deepened.

Finally, he broke the silence. "Maybe you should call your folks, Alfredo. They could meet us at the hospital." He reached across and handed Alfredo his cell phone. Alfredo took the phone from Chris' hand, but held off dialing. "You know...I don't think that I can do this, Chris. I say anything at all, I'm afraid I'm just gonna lose it, I can't have them hear me crying like a baby. I know, that's what'll happen."

Chris nodded. "Yeah, I know. But someone's gotta tell them. You just sit there and practice *out loud* a couple of times. You wanna cry, cry. I know! Practice and you'll get it right."

IX

As Chris and Alfredo pulled into the emergency vehicle parking area, they saw that the EMTs were already wheeling Mario into the ER. They could see as they ran toward the retreating stretcher that Mario hadn't moved — still wrapped in the woolen blanket, the breathing tube still exiting his mouth. An IV, hanging from a post, was dripping fluid into Mario's arm which now lay at his side outside of the blanket.

Alfredo shoved through the door and was met immediately by a heavy-set nurse. She gently laid a hand on Alfredo's shoulder, saying, "Okay, son. I know you're concerned. Ike told me you'd be here. You boys, just sit patiently and let us take care of things. We'll let you in to see your brother as soon as we can. But you have to let us take charge. Have the child's parents been notified?"

Chris, standing behind Alfredo, nodded and answered

for him. "Yes, ma'am, we called them on the way here. But we had to leave a message on the answering service. I hope they got the message. They should be here pretty soon."

"Good. Now I need to know just a few more things," the nurse said, beginning to take notes on her clipboard. "What's the young man's name? I think that Ike called him *Mario*, but we need to be sure. And how old is he? And we need *your* names, as well. And are you related to Mario?" she asked, looking at Alfredo.

Again, Chris answered, knowing that Alfredo was still too close to tears to risk speaking. "Yeah, his name's Mario—Mario Alhambra, ma'am. He's a freshman at Mission High—I guess he's about fourteen—that right, Alfredo?"

Alfredo nodded in affirmation, but did not speak.

"And this here's Alfredo Alhambra, Mario's brother. I'm Chris Battleson. We found him at Los Lobos—we think he's been there all night—someone tied him to his surfboard and left him there—on the beach."

The nurse stood there momentarily, staring at Chris, but did not say anything. Then nodding in the direction of both young men, she simply turned and, and tucking her clipboard under her arm, disappeared back into the ER. Alfredo quickly moved to the ER door and studied what action he could see through the windows of the swinging doors. Mario was now in a hospital bed. He could see a doctor talking with the EMTs as he checked Mario's signs. Somebody had replaced the IV and added at least one more. In fact, in the past few minutes, Mario had become a body swathed in wires and tubes.

Alfredo slowly turned to Chris, stared at him for a

minute. "This doesn't make any sense," he murmured. "I don't know what's happening. Why we're here!" He swung around to face the ER doors once more. "Someone's got to tell us, Chris, what the hell's going on? That's Littlebrother in there lying on that bed. He's got tubes everywhere! This isn't right!"

Alfredo, his face gone pale, grimaced and the look he shot Chris told it all: there was no easing the pain he was feeling. "I got to sit down. I think that I'm going to be sick!"

Chris simply shook his head and took Alfredo by the arm, leading him to the couch. "I'm going to get us some cokes. The machine's back there in the hall. We'll just sit here and wait it out. Together."

Alfredo slouched down onto the couch, burying his head in his hands on his knees. He nodded, and Chris turned to get the cokes. Looking back, he watched for a moment as Alfredo's shoulders shook perceptibly. Chris, angrily punching coins into the coke machine, wondered to himself. *What the hell can I do about this? Jesus! I don't know what to say! What do you say to make all this go away? I just don't know...*

He pulled the two cokes from the machine and walked back into the waiting room, popping the tops of the two cans as he did so. Nothing had changed. Alfredo was still sitting there his head between his hands resting on his knees. Chris bumped him on the shoulder with the coke can, and, as Alfredo raised his head, Chris pushed the ice-cold can against his forehead. "It's gonna be all right, Alfredo. It's just going to take some time. We can't do much more than wait—and pray. But Mario's in good hands now. They're gonna bring him around."

"Yeah," Alfredo mumbled. I know. You're right. I just need to know who did that to him. Who would tie Littlebrother to his surfboard like that? Nobody hates Mario that much! I just know it! He's such a little kid!"

Chris looked away...across the waiting room to the cheap pictures of flowers hanging on the wall. "I don't know, Alfredo," he said. "I really don't. And the terrible thing is I think *I do*. And I think that you do too...I just don't want to believe it. You know what I'm saying?"

"Hey, Chris, you've been good to me this morning. You know that. I don't know what I would've done if I'd been by myself when...uh...we found Mario. I think I'd have just lost it entirely. So, thanks—for this morning." Alfredo, for the first time, flashed a glimmer of a smile. "I guess I really needed you after all."

Chris returned the smile and stood up. "Hey, I don't know about you, but I can't just sit here. I got to stand up, walk around, just work off some of the tension in my back and legs. Meanwhile, maybe we ought to get to know each other better. I figure we're going to be here a while!" He walked across the waiting room to the three pictures, badly daubed reproductions of spring flowers. All were garishly, brightly, splashed in reds and oranges and yellows. The greens, as in leaves, were in very short supply. "Jesus," he said, "if they're going to have pictures, you'd think that they could get some better ones than these. They look like they came from a swap meet."

Alfredo laughed quietly. "Yeah. I noticed them. They're pretty awful. I'm planning on being an art major when I get out of Mission. I've been doing pictures ever since I can remember. So I know a little about art—and those," he laughed quietly again, "are not art."

"You paint? Dang, that's pretty cool." Chris had turned away from the pictures on the wall to face him. "I can't draw worth shit. I wish I could. Sometimes I just stare out at the sunset at Los Lobos and want so badly to save the beauty. I've tried to photograph sunsets, but it just isn't the same thing. A least, not with my skills. My pictures are, what you could call, *wannabes*!" He laughed and Alfredo laughed with him.

"Yeah, I know what you mean. I'm guess I lucky. I've been working at it for a long time." Alfredo stood up and walked toward the doors leading into the ER. "Actually, it was beach scenes and surfing that made me begin working with water colors," he said staring through the windows of the swinging doors. "Damn! I wish they'd come out here and tell us something. They've pulled the curtain over where they put Mario. I can't see a thing. Shit! Anyway, yeah. At first I tried beach scenes. But I wasn't too good with them. I still don't know why. Maybe I don't know enough. So then, I thought I'd concentrate on portraits. I had this theory that portraits were better if I got beneath the physical...you know? Kind of like portraits should try to get to the person behind the mask. That was my word...mask. What people hide behind." Alfredo paused a moment. "My cousin, Carlos, for example. He's this big, rough Mexican dude. He likes the image, I guess. But, that's not really him at all. When he smiles, his whole appearance changes. He just my big brother, after all, laughing with me, teasing me. But then, when somebody comes around, he puts on this face, it's kind of scary how he can intimidate people. And I have to admit: his mask is pretty convincing!"

Chris nodded. "Yeah. I guess we all kind of hide behind what we want everyone to see."

Alfredo looked over at Chris. "Yes! That's just it. So I thought I could paint what wasn't really apparent. I failed...miserably, actually. And Mario's the one who taught me that! I kept practicing on Mario, on his portrait...first in oils. Jesus, he hated it! Then I discovered that I was pretty good in charcoals. But all my tries just kept on looking pretty much like Mario. That's when I discovered that some people don't have masks. Mario doesn't." Alfredo's voice trailed off. He covered his eyes with the palms of his hands, speaking softly. "Some people don't need masks, I guess."

Chris walked over to stand beside Alfredo. "You want to try to get hold of your mom and dad again? Maybe one of them has a cell phone on. Or maybe your dad's back in his office now. There's got to be someone there who'll take a message now!"

"Yeah, I guess we should. We got to use yours though. I forgot to pull mine from the car. I guess I haven't been thinking much this morning! But first let me finish...about Mario. You know how he loves to surf? Well, I discovered, kind of by accident, that it really isn't surfing—It's the *ocean*. That's what surfing means to him. You watch him. He'll be out there when everyone else has called it quits. Like yesterday, I guess! Surf's died down. Nothing. And there's Mario...just out there stretched flat-out on his board out beyond any chance of catching a wave. Just floating away out there. I asked him once. He said that he was 'listening to the ocean breathe' That's what he said. "Just 'listening to the ocean breathe.' Jesus, what's he doing in *there*! He belongs to us, Chris!

He doesn't belong in there! He's *Littlebrother!*"

Chris nodded. "Yeah, Alfredo, I don't know. Lemme go get the cell phone. It's in the truck. You could call from in here." Chris disappeared behind the waiting room doors, thinking of the confusion that was going on inside — inside the ER, inside Alfredo's head. He glanced at his watch, and saw that the morning had disappeared along with the gloom of low clouds. It was almost lunch time at Mission. *Shit,* he thought. *I got to call Reeni. She doesn't know what the hell's going on.* He reached into the glove compartment and pulled out his cell phone, punching in her number as he did so.

She answered immediately, asking, "Chris, where the heck are you? I've been trying to call you all morning! Are you all right???"

Chris, trying to keep his voice level, said, "Now just hold on, Reeni. Yeah, I'm all right. But things aren't." He then continued to relate to her the events of his morning, ending with the news that he and Alfredo were at the hospital waiting for word on Mario's condition."

"Ari...was *Aron* involved in this?" she asked. "I saw him for a moment this morning before first period. He was acting really strange."

"I don't know..." Chris answered. "But I think so. It kind of adds up, doesn't it. And it sucks! He was supposed to be my best friend. I – we really don't know what happened."

Reeni paused before answering, paused so long that Chris asked into the cell phone, "Reeni, you still there?"

Reeni answered, "Yes, I'm here. I was just thinking. Hey, I'm here at school. I bought lunch at the cafeteria when I couldn't find you. I'm coming to the hospital. I'll be there as soon as I can. Okay?"

"Yeah...Reeni, I need to have you here. Alfredo's not dealing with this shit. So, yeah. Come on. I'll see you when you get here!"

Chris signed off and redialed Alfredo's parents' number even as he hurried back into the waiting room. It was still ringing when he handed the phone over to Alfredo.

Lunchtime at Mission High School began with the usual exodus of seniors to the *Villager*. Aron had noticed the absence of Chris before school in the parking lot. He wondered idly where Chris might be – it wasn't much like him to miss school. And being locked away in the Detention Center, he wondered...and was beginning to worry. He'd tried to talk to Reeni at the mid-morning break, but she wasn't saying much to him. In fact, she pretty much gave him the old cold shoulder. Still, she hadn't seemed terribly concerned...And he hated the isolation of the Detention Center. He was used to the camaraderie of his classmates both during classes and at the breaks between periods.

And Reenie wasn't concerned. She had decided that, after their meeting yesterday afternoon with Father Leo, Chris was probably getting set for tonight's confrontation.

And *confrontation* she'd decided was really the only honest word to describe what she and Chris were both dreading! Still, she trusted him. Chris could take care of himself, and she was sure that she'd see him by lunchtime. Thus, when she didn't find him in the parking lot at lunchtime—their usual plan—she began to grow concerned. She found her own car and called him on her cell phone. No answer. She knew that he kept his own cell phone in his truck during school hours, so she figured that he wasn't in his truck. *Oh, well. He'll show up!* she thought.

Aron, meanwhile, was out of the Detention Center and ordering lunch at the *Villager*. He'd paid and was carrying his tray to one of the outdoor tables when he was confronted—three hefty Mexicans, two about his own age, the third somewhat older had surrounded him. The largest of the three, Carlos, stood directly in front of him, blocking his path; the other two came up on his left and right, shoulders pushing slightly inward against Aron.

"Aron Levin, right?" Carlos had put his fist squarely in Aron's chest.

Aron looked up into the tall Mexican's dark eyes. "Hey, pal," he said, "you want to get your fucking hand off me and get out of my way?"

"No. And don't call me 'pal.' I'm not *your pal*. I just might be your worst nightmare, you little *cretino*. Before you begin your lunch, you need to know. We're on your back. We're like the *moscas* that gnaw at your eyelids. You know what *moscas* are? Probably not, you dumb shit. But you're gonna find out. My two friends here—the ones on your right and left: Take a good look at them,

Levin. You're gonna be seeing a lot of them in the next couple of days—maybe weeks. But make no mistakes— They're not your *amigachos*. "

Then, giving Aron a quick jab with his fist and deliberately knocking Aron's lunch from his hands, Carlos and his two buddies, turned and walked back to their car. Geoff and Buddy, Aron's surfing buddies, had joined him to watch as the three drove off. Carlos' Ford Bronco was cherry red and impeccably clean. And Carlos was purposeful in his leave-taking: slow, decisive.

"What was that all about, Ari," Geoff asked. "Jesus, he even dumped your lunch. Who was that?"

"I don't have a clue," Ari answered, watching the Bronco turn left onto the highway back toward town. "But he sure thought he was some tough shit."

"Well, yeah...I suspect he *is* as tough as he thinks, if you ask me. What the hell did you do to him?"

"Don't ask me...Probably sometime to do with that little spic – what's his name? Mario! He's probably got a whole gang of *spics* on my case. Oh, well. They don't belong...and they know it! It's no big deal. I got to get some more lunch. Don't sweat it, I'm not going to!"

XI

"This is my Dad and Ma," Alfredo nodded toward Chris, as he went to meet a middle-aged couple hurrying across the waiting room from the entry. Alfredo met his mother's open arms, as she cried, "What's happened, Freddie? Where's Mario?" Mrs. Alhambra pushed Alfredo back to look up into his face. She reached with narrow long fingers to tenderly brush tears from her son's cheeks, saying, "Tell me. What's happened?"

She stepped back to look up into Alfredo's face. Wearing a pair of designer jeans, a small-print flowered silk blouse, and a camel-hair jacket, she appeared to be a young woman whose self-assured presence was in control of almost any situation. Her short-cut, curly black hair framed her softly-featured face and lent a kind of warmth to her countenance. If she was scared, Chris thought, one could detect it in her voice, not in her manner.

Mr. Alhambra had taken Alfredo by his upper arm and gently pulled him around. "Mario—he's in there?" he said, gesturing toward the ER and making it sound more like a statement than a question. Alfredo nodded. And Mr. Alhambra turned and strode toward the swinging doors. He was met immediately by an orderly who discreetly, but firmly, blocked his way.

"I'm Richard Alhambra...You've got my son, Mario, in there." Again, he spoke as if it were a statement of fact rather than a question. "I want to see him; I need to see the doctor."

Like his wife, Mr. Alhambra was younger-looking than he surely was. In fact, Chris might have mistaken him for Alfredo's older brother except for the tinges of grey that were brushed into his wavy black hair. Dressed in a business suit, he, too, looked as if he were in charge. And, indeed, his manner was straight up and fully self-possessed. He, too, managed to exhibit publicly little of the tension that must have been moving irresponsibly through his body.

The orderly, pausing momentarily, stepped aside, saying, "The ER staff is working with Mario right now, sir, but if you'll just wait a moment, I'll tell Dr. Jamison that you're out here. Then he can take you in to see Mario. But, I'm sure that he'd rather talk to you first. Just give me a couple of minutes to get him, to tell him that you're here and that you would like to speak with him." With that, he turned and disappeared behind the doors.

Mr. Alhambra turned back to Alfredo. "You didn't say much in your phone message...just that Mario had been hurt and was here at the hospital. So, what happened?"

Alfredo stammered out an explanation, relating how he and Chris had gone searching for Mario, had found him tied to his surf board at Los Lobos, had called 911, and had "followed the EMTs here to the ER."

Mr. Alhambra stared at Alfredo for several uninterrupted seconds, before exploding, "Tied to his surfboard??? What the hell are you talking about, Fredo?"

"Just that, Daddy. That's how me and Chris found him…"

"I don't understand what you are saying at all! And this, I guess, is Chris?" Mr. Alhambra asked, glancing in Chris's direction.

"Oh, yeah, I'm sorry, Daddy. I forgot. Chris, this is my Dad and Ma, Mr. and Mrs. Alhambra. Daddy, Ma. This is Chris Battleson."

"Yes, well—"

These introductions were short-circuited by the arrival of a doctor through the swinging doors. All four turned to face him as he introduced himself as "Dr. Jamison, Will Jamison. I've been looking after young Mario since he arrived here this morning," he said. He looked from Alfredo to Mario's parents before continuing. "Let me give you a quick rundown of where we are. Mario was—"

"Just tell me how Mario is, "Mrs. Alhambra interrupted.

Dr. Jamison gently motioned with his hand, saying, "Please, Mrs. Alhambra. I know how worried you are. Let me tell you where we are right now, and then I hope to be able to answer most of your questions.

"Mario was brought into the ER in a coma. He was, is, suffering from an advanced hypothermia. Which means that his body has shut down in reaction to the cold and the wet that he experienced during what was, as I understand it, his night on the beach." Jamison paused, looked at all four members of his audience. When no one replied to his implied question, he continued. "We don't know the extent of damage to his system. His heart is strong. He's breathing, but on a respirator, so we don't really know the extent of damage to his lungs. And, of course, there is the potential of brain damage. We haven't done a CAT-scan yet. We need to be sure that Mario is stabilized. And, to be frank, he really isn't stabilized…"

Mr. Alhambra, wiping away a tear from his eye, reached over to the doctor's arm. "Tell me—us, up front. What are Mario's chances. You haven't given us much…"

"Mr. Alhambra," Jamison said. "I think that we can be cautiously optimistic. Now, I know that's a term that people throw around, but it's the best I can do right now. I'd be lying if I said that Mario was on his way to recovery. We just don't know. We do know that his condition…the coma…is his body's way of reacting to the stress that last night put on him. You should probably know that we have notified the Sheriff about all this. They're going to want to know *why* Mario spent the night on the beach.

"So, if you will to come with me, you can see him. But, I want to warn you: don't expect too much: He's in a coma. He may hear you talking to him, but he probably won't react to anything you say."

With that, Dr. Jamison turned and opened the swinging doors leading into the ER. Ricardo and Elena Alhambra followed in the direction that he had motioned. He then paused as Alfredo followed his mother. "Could you wait just a moment, Alfredo? You could go in after your parents have had their visit with young Mario. Okay?"

Alfredo nodded and turned sullenly back to Chris. "I guess I can wait," he mumbled and slumped once more on the couch in the waiting room. "Shit. It's all I've done for the past several hours!"

Chris reached over a pulled a straight-back chair to sit facing Alfredo. He gripped Alfredo's knee in his fisted hand. "I know that it doesn't sound good right now, buddy, but it's early. They'll pull him through. They know what they're doing in there. You got to hold on to that. And, Alfredo, look at me...When you do get in there, you just walk in and you just start talking to him...Be positive, just talk to him, tell him that you love him...anything! I know he'll hear you!"

"I know. I know! I just don't know if I can handle seeing him...like we saw him on the beach. That was different, you know? We had things to do. Now, it's all so friggin' helpless." Alfredo looked away again, before cupping his face in his hands.

"We'll just hang in there, Alfredo...Give some of your strength to Mario. You can do it." Chris tapped Alfredo on the shoulder. "Hey, your mom calls you Freddie," he laughed. "I think that's cool!"

Alfredo looked up smiling. "Yeah. She always has. Daddy, him and Mario call me Fredo—well, almost everyone in our family does. But, Ma, she's called me Freddie ever since I can remember. Must come from our being *Americanized*!" Alfredo continued to smile, seeing that Chris caught the gentle sarcasm of his words. "She can, but ain't nobody else! So don't even try!" Alfredo said pushing Chris backward with the palm of his hand on Chris's shoulder. Chris turned to pick up his coke can.

Alfredo paused a moment before he, again, abruptly stood up. "Dang! They're taking a long time in there. This is all *too hard*, Chris." He walked over to the swinging doors, but turned back immediately realizing that he could see nothing. Walking toward the doors leading to the outside, he stared out into the sunshine. "Well, at least the friggin' fog burned off. How long have we been here, anyway, Chris?"

Chris looked at his watch. "About three hours or so, I guess. I don't know exactly when we got here, but it's past noon. I wonder where Reeni is. She said she was coming down here."

Even as he stood there looking out into the parking areas, Alfredo watched a Sheriff's patrol car slow to a stop in one of the emergency room's parking spaces. "I think we are in for another get-together, Chris," Alfredo said, inspecting the vehicle and the two deputies who were emerging from it.

"Whaddaya mean," Chris said, rising from the chair. "What's happening out there?"

"Sheriff's here."

"Oh." Chris moved to the door to stand next to Alfredo. They watched as the deputies stood at the rear of their patrol car, talking. If they had seen to the two young men at the door, which they assuredly had, they gave no indication of it. Chris, nudging Alfredo's shoulder, moved back into the interior of the waiting room. "We might as well make ourselves comfortable. And Alfredo, we don't pull any punches. If Ari's behind this, he's no friend of mine. You got that? It's Mario. He's the one that needs us now. Okay?"

Alfredo turned from the doorway. "Yeah. I know. And I know what you're saying. I really do. But I also know that I found a friend this morning. We're going to be okay. Right?"

The two sheriff's deputies came through the door together, one carrying a small pad in his right hand. The other sheriff approached the two young men saying, "Good morning, gentlemen. I take it one of you is Alfredo Alhambra?"

Alfredo half-raised his hand in a quick recognition of his name and nodded at the deputies.

"I guess you know why we are here. I'm Deputy Thad Richter. This is my partner, Deputy Karl Iverson. The ER Staff called us—they said they told you guys that we would be called. Right? And they gave us some background information, too."

Both of the boys nodded. "Good," he continued, "then, let's just begin with some preliminaries. I take it that you, Alfredo, are Mario's brother?"

"I am, sir," Alfredo stood forward, reaching over to shake the deputy's hand.

"And you are Chris, right? I think that we've met," Richter said, looking over at Chris.

"Chris Battleson, sir. I'm…ummm, going with your niece, Reeni Richter. I'm with Alfredo. He's my friend. We're the ones who found Mario and called 911."

"Okay. Well, since we've started, let's get to the facts here. Why don't we all take a seat. Deputy Iverson here is going to take some notes. I'll ask most of the questions." Alfredo slumped back onto the couch; Chris sat in his chair. The deputies continued to stand, deliberately apart from them so as not to appear threatening.

"Now. You two found Mario at Los Lobos. Right?" Richter looked from Chris to Alfredo.

Both boys nodded, and Richter went on. "Fine. What we both want to know is why Los Lobos? What were you thinking?"

Chris looked over and nodded at Alfredo who appeared to be examining a small speck of dust in the corner of the room. He smiled slightly and took a deep breath. "Well," Alfredo began, "when Mario didn't show up at school this morning, I kind of got worried. Then, I found out that he *hadn't* spent the night with his buddy, we thought he had. And his buddy, Bobby, told me that they had quit surfing late yesterday afternoon, but that Mario had stayed at Los Lobos to surf some more. So, me and Chris just decided to go there. We checked the house first—thinking Mario maybe was there, that maybe he had overslept. He wasn't there."

Alfredo paused, staring off into space. Richter waited, and, deciding that Alfredo had finished whatever he was going to say, asked, "So you're at Los Lobos. Then what?"

"Well, we…uh…we decided to search the beach. We found Mario's bike there. So we knew something was up. And it was." Again, Alfredo paused, this time staring at Richter momentarily. "We found Mario—Chris did. He was lying on his back…tied to his surfboard…" Alfre paused again, clearing his throat. His eyes again tear over. He dropped his head into his han

Chris turned to Iverson and Richter
go on. I—we found Mario. He wasn'

That was pretty obvious. We covered him up with our shirts and a blanket and called 911. Ike and his buddy got there, and they pretty much took over. That's about it..."

Deputy Iverson, who had been scribbling notes as both Alfredo and Chris described their morning, said, "You guys did the all the right things. But I'm not clear on one thing. Mario was tied to his surfboard. What do you mean *tied to his surfboard*? Tied, how?"

"Uh...well, he had these bungee cords that were strapped across his chest and looped his arms around the bottom of the board. The same for his feet. The bungee cord tied his legs—his ankles—to the bottom of the board. He was lying on his back. The tide was beginning to go out, so the sand was still kind of piled around the board and over his ankles. He couldn't move." Chris looked over at Alfredo who hadn't looked up during this recital. His shoulders were visibly trembling.

Deputy Richter moved over to pat Alfredo on his shoulder. "I know this is tough, son, but we have to get some things straight here. So, please just bear with us. We'll make this a quick and as easy as we possibly can." He looked over at Iverson and nodded his head.

Deputy Iverson cleared his throat. "Okay. You two guys got any ideas. I mean, I know it's not easy." He paused then taking a deep breath continued. "Mario didn't just show up tied to his board at Los Lobos. So what's your take on the deal?"

Alfredo looked up and started to speak before Chris motioned to him. "No. Lemme handle this, Fredo." He paused and looked over at Richter. "Yeah. We've – I've got an idea. There's this kid at school. He kind of has it in or...uh..."

"Go ahead, Chris," Alfredo interrupted him. "We got to get this out in the open. "What Chris wants to say is *"spicsI"* And he can't. And Chris...thanks for caring. But that's the word, officers. *Spics*. That's what this guy called us. Me and Mario."

"When?" Iverson asked. "When did this happen?" He spoke through a noticeably tightened jaw.

"Well, first off, Sunday afternoon. When Mario and I came in from surfing. Chris heard him." Alfredo looked over at Chris, and Chris nodded in confirmation and continued, "Yeah. I heard the whole thing. I was there," he said. "But it happened again. This time I saw what happened. This kid comes up to Mario at lunch time and sucker-punches him and calls him the name again. In front of a lot of kids, too."

"So *this kid*, you say, called both you and Mario this name," Richter repeated looking at Alfredo. "Do either of you two want to tell us the name of this creep? I mean, so far, he's *this kid*. So far as I know, we've been dodging the obvious. I *want* a name. What do you say?" Richter's words were strong, but his tone of voice matched the sympathy that he was feeling for these two young men.

Again, Chris held up his hand. "No, Fredo. This is my call. I'm the one who saw both of the incidents. Okay, sir, here's the deal. His name is Aron Levin...and until Sunday afternoon, he was my best friend. And he quit being that big time when I saw him go after Mario yesterday at lunch. I don't know what's happened to him. But he's way wrong, sir. And he hates the idea of guys like Mario and Alfredo surfing what he thinks of as *his* waves."

"You agree with this assessment," Richter asked

looking over at Alfredo.

Alfredo nodded, affirming Chris' description. "Yes, sir, I think that it's pretty much as Chris says. Levin's attitude was pretty ugly at Los Lobos. We totally weren't expecting him to go off on us. Then, when I heard about what happened to Mario yesterday, well, I just didn't know what to do. But I figured that the school had a handle on it. I know Mr. Beck called Levin into his office. So I figured I'd better let things ride and see how—"

Richter signaled Alfredo to hold up for a moment. "Okay. Well, here's what we'd like from you both. You just continue to 'let things ride,' as you say. You just understand that we can handle things from here on out. It's our job...the ball's in our court. And Alfredo...Chris. Trust us. We're just as offended by this Aron Levin's language as you are. And, yes, the school will have its say...but so will the Sheriff's Department. That kind of language is simply intolerable. Period. We'll take care of this from here on out."

Deputy Richter stood and reached across to shake hands first with Alfredo, then with Chris. Deputy Iverson did likewise, saying, "And thanks, you two, for your honesty. We need this kind of honesty if we are to do our job. You'll be. hearing from us!"

"Hey, Officer Richter, before you go." Chris followed the two deputies toward the ER doors. "There's one other thing you should know. Aron has a canvas bag in his truck with a couple—maybe four bungee cords..."

Chris and Alfredo watched in silence as the two deputies left the waiting room; both passed through the swinging doors into the Emergency Room. Richter appeared within moments in the parking lot by the squad car.

Alfredo turned to Chris and smiled openly for the first time. "Thanks Chris. I really needed your support there for a minute. And…You know how much I appreciated your calling me *Fredo*?

Chris looked back at Alfredo, smiling. "Hey. We're in this together. We gotta be, now. And I wasn't kidding, Fredo. Ari's not my friend. His style just isn't my way…I guess it never was. I was just too stupid to see it – or at least see it for what it really is…"

XII

Reeni pulled into the emergency room parking lot as the deputies stopped in front of their car. "Hey, Uncle Thad, what're you guys doing here?" she yelled, as she ran over to hug her uncle; It was a gesture that Deputy Richter hated when he was in uniform. Reeni knew, but she did it anyway – knowing, but still too fond of her uncle to follow the rules of the road.

"Well, now that you ask. We've been in talking to *your* Chris and his buddy, Alfredo Alhambra. They've had quite a morning—saving Alfredo's younger brother. Why don't you all go on in there. I think Chris has been waiting for you!" Richter hugged his niece quickly and gently shoved her toward the waiting room. Iverson, meanwhile, had returned to the patrol car from the ER entrance and was checking his cell phone for messages.

Sliding into the driver's seat, he belted himself in as

Karl Iverson did likewise. "Why don't you get on the phone and call Sam Beck at the high school. We're going to need to see him and this Levin dude."

"I'm already on this. By the way, you know who he is?" Iverson asked as he reached for his cell phone. "This Levin kid? His dad's the City Attorney. That fact just might color a lot of where we are going with this. We're going to have to talk to young Levin without his lawyer-dad present?"

Richter looked over at his partner smiling. "Hey. We're just following department policy. Just following leads. Anyway, what did you find out? How's the kid doing?"

"Not well at all. His parents are still in there, looking pretty grim. The doctor, Jamison's still on duty. He didn't sound even a little positive. Seems they can't get the kid to breathe on his own. Don't have much of a take on his brain activity, either."

"Jesus," Richter swore under his breath. "This is getting to sound worse and worse. I sure as hell hope we don't have a homicide on our hands. Alhambra—he's no light-weight around town either. Know who he is?"

"Yup. City Manager. Very old Dos Padres Valley family. But I just put it together. This is altogether not cool. The City Attorney's kid goes after the City Manager's kid?"

"And," Richter added, "one's brown and one's white. How's that for complicating things?" Iverson nodded over to his partner. He wasn't smiling. "Well, you'd better dial up Beck. We gotta start somewhere and Mission High seems the somewhere right now," Richter concluded.

Iverson did so, and reached Beck immediately. Richter listened in as he made arrangements to meet with Beck and, immediately afterwards, to meet with Aron Levin.

XIII

As Reeni passed through the waiting room doors, she saw Alfredo disappear into the ER. Chris approached her, holding out his hands. She grasped both of his hands in hers, asking, "Chris, what's this all about? What happened to Mario? Uncle Thad said something about you and Alfredo saving his life?"

Chris led her toward the couch, repeating one more time the events of the morning, adding that the ER nurse had just called Alfredo into see Mario. "His parents have been in there with Mario for about a half hour or more. We really don't know much yet. Just that Mario is pretty much in a coma...but the doctor, Dr. Jamison, says that that's the kind of thing the body does – kind of to protect itself from shock and pain. The body just shuts down. So that's about it."

"And you think that Ari has something to do with all this?"

"Shit, I don't know…" Chris paused, staring out over Reeni's shoulder into the parking lot. "I don't want to think that he could do something this awful! He was my friend. How could I have been so blind to this side of him? Jesus! He was my buddy!"

Reeni pushed away from Chris, putting her hand on his cheek. "Wait!" she cried. "Wait just a minute. You're not responsible for what happened to Mario! You saved him! Uncle Thad said so!"

"Yeah, I know…" Chris said putting his hand over Reeni's. "But…You know…Alfredo and I were talking just a minute ago about the masks that people wear. I keep thinking about the mask that Ari wears sometimes. I mean…I think that I know him, but now I guess I don't know him all. I mean, he sucker-punched Mario yesterday in front of me and you and all those other kids, and he didn't bat an eyelash. Like he hadn't done anything wrong! I just didn't know that side of Ari. And…well, I guess maybe I was just stupid. How come I never saw it, Reeni?" He continued to stare beyond her into vacant space.

"Hey, Christo! I thought I knew him, too! I didn't see that side of Ari either. You *cannot* blame yourself!" Reeni reached up to put her hands on Chris' shoulders. "It's not you!"

"Okay! I guess I'm not blaming myself. I'm just kind of…well…kind of screwed up!" Chris paused for a minute, before continuing. "Here's the good news! Alfredo's a very cool guy. He's pretty up-front…you know, honest!"

Chris walked to the doorway and, looking out, said, "Reeni, we still on for meeting with Father Leo and our parents tonight?"

Reeni paused before answering. "Well, yes, I guess so. I guess I'm just trying to figure out how all this plays into tonight. But, yes, we have to go through with tonight's meeting."

Chris had no chance to answer, for he first heard rather than saw Alfredo and his parents pushing through the swinging doors from the ER. They moved slowly, grimly into the waiting room. No one said anything for what seemed to Chris to be minutes.

Elena Alhambra moved woodenly toward one of the couches. She was supported on both sides by her husband and son. Ricardo Alhambra, his jaw so tightly shuttered that the muscles along his jawbone seemed rigidly, permanently flexed. His composure, as before, was in check, though now it appeared to be a mockery of his earlier self-possession.

Elena Alhambra stood momentarily before the couch, staring downward, seemingly undecided as to whether she should sit. Then, abruptly deciding against any sign of weakness, she turned to touch Alfredo on his cheek. "We'll get through this, Freddie," she said softly. "We have no choice." Her efforts at her earlier self-assurance barely concealed her anxiety.

She turned away and walked quickly to the doorway leading to the parking lot. Staring out the window, she watched as Carlos jumped out of his Bronco and ran toward the door. Opening the door for him, she reached out to hug her nephew, burying her head in his shoulder. Mr. Alhambra quickly crossed the room to reach Carlos and take him by the arm. "Carlitos. Thanks for coming. You know about Mario? About what happened?"

'Not much, Uncle Ricardo. Some of it. Just that it's something to do with Mario? He okay?" Carlos looked intently across the room and nodded bleakly to Alfredo.

Mr. Alhambra looked away, then turned to Alfredo and his wife. "Not well, I guess you could say. Carlitos," he continued, but still not looking in his direction, "they aren't saying much in there, but they're not offering any encouragement, either. Mario's condition, well…is more than serious. They are moving him to the Intensive Care Unit right about now, or soon, anyway. But, I guess I don't know what to say from here…" Mr. Alhambra's voice trailed off. "I guess we just have to wait."

Elena Alhambra stepped up to take her husband's arm. "They, well, Dr. Jamison, said that they've done a brain scan on Mario. The nearest they can come to a diagnosis at this point is that Mario suffered a serious decrease of oxygen to his brain." She paused, trembling, to take a deep breath, to reestablish a kind of control over her voice, before continuing. "He's comatose, Carlitos — except that he does have infrequent muscle spasms. He's on life-support still. What they are really saying, but not actually saying, is that Mario's condition is irreversible. There's not much brain activity evident from the CAT Scan."

Carlos moved away from his aunt and uncle, coming up to his cousin, said, "Hey, Fredo, you gonna be okay?" He took Alfredo into his arms, drawing him close. Alfredo, at first numb, dropped his head to Carlos' shoulder and stood there, quietly trembling.

"No, Carlitos. Nothing's okay. I just don't understand."

"I'm here. We'll get through this together, Fredo." Carlos looked around at Chris and Reeni who had moved back and out of the way of the family. "Who are your friends, Fredo?"

Alfredo turned, half-apologizing. "Oh, yeah. Carlitos, this is Chris...Chris Battleson. He's really been a friend this morning," he said, almost too quietly, and halting momentarily before adding, "Chris, this is my cousin, Carlos Alvarez. And, Reeni—Gee, I'm sorry, I don't know your last name, but Carlitos, this is Reeni; she's with Chris." Alfredo did not look at anyone during these introductions.

Shaking hands with Reeni, Carlitos looked carefully at Chris. "You help my cousin here, and you become my friend as well," he said, but there was little friendliness in his voice. The mask was on.

Alfredo, meanwhile, had turned back toward his parents, looking first at his mother, then his father. "Daddy, where do we go from here? I mean...what are we supposed to do?"

Mr. Alhambra smiled grimly, looking over at his wife. "We just hang loose here. They've probably moved Mario to ICU. We'll go up there to be with him. But beyond that, Alfredo, I guess we just wait and see what Dr. Jamison is thinking. I don't see that we have any other options. But...I do think that we have got to prepare ourselves. Nothing looks too good right now..." Mr. Alhambra broke off, his voice trembling. There were tears forming in the corners of his eyes.

Alfredo's mother stared at her husband and son, waiting for one or the other to speak. When neither of them did, she came forward to take Alfredo by the arm. "Freddy," she asked, "where's the Mustang? Is it still at school?"

Alfredo shook his head. "Yeah, I guess Chris has been ferrying me around."

Elena Alhambra turned. "Well, Chris, I've got one more favor to ask of you." The effort to speak, to control small pieces of their trauma, was evident in her tremulous voice. "Could you *ferry* Alfredo one more time? To the high school? To get his car?"

"Sure thing, Mrs. Alhambra," Chris said. "We can do that." He paused to find Alfredo who had moved behind his father to stand with Carlos. "You want to go now, Alfredo?" he asked. "You can be back here in fifteen, twenty minutes." He looked over at Alfredo who nodded and returned Chris's gaze, but saw nothing.

Chris continued, if only to hold at bay the silence that continued to fall on the waiting room. "Reeni can follow us in her car. Okay, Reeni?"

Reeni nodded her assent and moved toward the door. Alfredo bent over to kiss his mother on the cheek. "I'll be back soon, Ma," he murmured. "Carlitos," he said, "you wanna wait here 'til I get back?"

Carlos looked across the waiting room at his cousin, his eyes registering both his assent and his overwhelming sorrow…for his aunt and uncle, for his cousin, his friend, his brother, for the whole cheerless ordeal.

XIV

In fact, Sam Beck was waiting for the two deputies on this Tuesday afternoon when they arrived and, greeting them both by name, immediately escorted them into his office. Samuel Beck was a tall man, athletic looking, and dressed today in conservative grey trousers and a navy blazer. His white, button-down dress shirt was complemented by a muted blue-and-grey striped tie. In his mid-forties, Beck had been a teacher and counselor before moving into an administrative position at Mission. Having been the dean for discipline for the past four years, he was beginning to feel the itch of cynicism and depression that comes with the day-to-day monitoring of student misbehavior. And because of his position as dean of discipline, he had worked with both deputies on a fairly regular basis. He knew and respected Thad Richter and Karl Iverson for their integrity and their patient understanding of both student misconduct and the high school's concern for student privacy.

Sam Beck, in his efforts to ensure balance in his life at Mission High coached soccer in season, first because he like the sport, but even more because coaching gave him an essential chance to deal with students in an entirely different and mostly positive atmosphere. Getting away from behind his desk afforded him the refreshing opportunity to interact with his students in a physical and emotional interplay of tough athletic competition as well as to share with his players his own keen sense of competition and will to win.

"This doesn't sound too good, you guys," he began, as he motioned to the deputies to sit. Beck stood behind his desk. "I don't know what's up, but I have a bad feeling about this. Karl tells me that you want to see Aron Levin. Did you know that I had him in here just yesterday afternoon? He's on a three-day in-house suspension even as we sit here."

Richter shifted slightly in his seat. "Well, Sam, here's where we are…Mario Alhambra is probably in the ICU by this time at Los Lobos Hospital. In critical condition…" The deputy then continued to sort through the events as Chris and Alfredo had related them. He ended with the young men naming Aron Levin as a possible cause of Mario's circumstances.

"And they told you about the *spic* incident," Beck said. It was not a question. "That's what we suspended Levin for. And he didn't even deny what he had said and done. Actually, when I spoke with his father, Mr. Levin seemed more angry about the suspension than about his kid's language! Jesus! And his father's a friggin' attorney." Beck smiled grimly.

"Yeah," Iverson joined in, "and a co-worker with Mario's father. Mr. Alhambra's the City Manager."

"Yeah, I know all about that!" Beck said. "Okay, here's the deal. We've got Aron Levin down in the Counseling Conference Room. You could interview him there. You want me on-board for this?"

Deputy Richter looked over at his partner, who nodded and said, "Yes, if you've got the time, Sam. We've got to be pretty careful here. I don't relish playing legal tag with Aron Levin's old man."

Beck nodded and smiled. 'Yeah, I got all the time in the world!" he said sardonically. He picked up Aron's discipline folder from his in-basket, walked around his desk to led the two deputies down the hall to the Counseling Conference Room. Opening the door, he saw Aron Levin slouched in a captain's chair at the conference table. Beck held the door open as Richter and Iverson entered the room and took the captain's chairs opposite Aron at the table. Beck seated himself at the head of the table before introducing both deputies to Aron Levin. Aron, rolling his eyes upward, merely nodded at the introductions.

Deputy Richter, watching Aron closely, chose to ignore the student's insulting manner and began the meeting, trying to sound both routine and friendly. "Good afternoon, Aron. Deputy Iverson and I are here to begin to make some sense of a problem that has arisen. And we thought that you might be able to give us some insights. Do you mind answering a few simple questions?"

Aron sat up straight in his chair, staring smugly, first at Beck and than at Richter. "No," he replied, "not at all.

Anyway, I don't really have much of a choice, do I? I mean, look at you guys. We got the disciplinarian and two sheriff's deputies here."

"Well, good then," Richter answered, again ignoring Aron's pretty obvious attempts at striking an attitude. "First off, we'd like to know how well-acquainted you are with Mario and Alfredo Alhambra. You know these two young men?"

Aron smirked. "Yeah...I know who they are. But that's about it. They go here to school. I know who they are. That okay with you?" He added, belligerently.

"Well, gee, Aron. That's fine. I guess my next question is just as simply answered. We understand that you are presently serving a three-day in-house suspension. Mind telling us what this is all about?"

Aron looked around and found Iverson taking notes in his notebook. "If this is all so friendly," he asked, "what's that guy taking notes for? You guys trying to pin something on me?"

"Uh, no, not really," Richter answered. "Deputy Iverson is taking notes because that's what we do. We like to make sure that we know the substance of any interview we take. We don't make mistakes when we have notes to rely on. But getting back to the question..."

Aron began slouching again into his seat. "It's a dumb question, Mr. Richter. You already know what I'm in for. Mario badmouthed me in front of my friends, and I slugged him one. No big deal. He asked for it, I gave it to him. It was that simple."

"Well, first off, Aron, I'm not Mr. Richter. I'm Deputy Richter. You need to get that straight. Next, Mr. Beck is here because we need him to read the substance of your suspension. Mr. Beck?"

Sam Beck opened the folder in front of him on the desk and read the notes he had taken from the meetings, first with students he had talked with right after the incident, then with Mario; he related his conversation with Aron Levin, concluding with the notes from his conversation with Aron's father.

"So, there isn't much evidence in that report, based on your fellow students' descriptions of the event, that Mario was badmouthing you," Richter began. "In fact, as Mr. Beck reports, you even admit that it was a 'sucker-punch.' A backfisted smack to the side of Mario's head — Mario wasn't even facing you. That right?"

"Whatever you say, *sir*," Aron said.

"And you called him a foul name, too. That's also correct?" Richter continued.

"I didn't call him no foul name. I just called him by a name he would recognize. *Spic*. There's no doubt he recognized his name when I used it! You gonna arrest me for calling it like I see it?" Aron smirked again, seeming to believe he had gotten the upper hand.

"Yeah. Well, whatever you believe, you should know that *Spic* is a detestable name – degrading, deliberately offensive, *ugly*." Richter leaned back in his chair for a moment, surveying Aaron across the table from him. Aron met his gaze fleetingly then quickly looked away.

"When was the last time you saw either of the two brothers—you remember?" This question came from Deputy Iverson who had looked up from his notes. He had watched as his partner remained silent, before nodding in his direction.

"Uh…I don't exactly remember. I guess I saw Alfredo

the last time surfing on Sunday at Los Lobos. Mario...well, you already figured that one out. Yesterday afternoon – at lunchtime," Aron countered looking up defiantly.

"Okay," Richter continued. "Could you please tell us where you were yesterday afternoon?"

Aron looked back down at his hands which were clenched on the table top. "Yeah," he answered. "I was surfing with my friends, Geoff and Buddy. That okay with you? Should I have asked your permission?"

"No, of course not," Richter said, again smiling. "As I said, we are just trying to figure out a situation here. How about last evening, Aron. Where were you last night?"

"Home. I was working on my surfboard. In my garage. You could ask my dad, he'll tell you."

"Yes. I'm sure he will. Thanks for your honesty." Deputy Richter looked over at his partner before continuing. "Uh, Aron," Richter asked suddenly. "You own any bungee cords—like, maybe, stashed in your car? We heard that you have a small satchel with maybe three or four bungee cords that you keep in the trunk of your car. That right?"

"Shit!" Aron spat out the word. It remained in the air for several seconds as neither deputy nor Beck reacted to his expletive. "So now you got Chris Battleson on my case too. What is this? Some kind of fucking inquisition? Yeah, I got bungee cords. So what? Is that some sort of crime?"

"No, no, no..." Richter said gently. "No. We're just interested—just as we said at the outset. We're just clearing up some loose ends here. Maybe we could take a quick look-see?"

Sam Beck raised his hand, palm forward, nodding to Thad Richter. "Please, Deputy Richter. I need to say something at this point. Okay?"

Richter nodded in assent, and Sam Beck waited silently until Aron looked over at him before continuing. "Aron. I think that you are well aware of language restrictions on the campus. I will not tolerate your casual use of expletives in this conference room or anywhere on this campus. One more outburst from you with language like that and you'll no longer be facing an in-house suspension. You'll be up before an expulsion board. You understand?"

Aron stared down at the table. He concurred with a slight shaking of his head. However, his body language was such that Mr. Beck was sure that he didn't understand *at all*.

"So," Richter continued, "how about we take a quick look at your vehicle and the bungee cords?"

"Now?" Aron sat up straight once again. "You wanna see my bungee cords right now?"

"Well, yes. That's what we'd like. Unless you have some objection..."

Again, Richter had taken on a gentle tone and allowed a slight smile to cross his face. He stood as did Iverson and Beck. All three waited for Aron Levin to stand as well. But he sat there for several seconds, staring defiantly at the two deputies. Finally, he lifted himself slowly out of his chair. Sam Beck moved to the door and held it open for the deputies and Aron Levin. Thad Richter then led the party out through the Attendance Office doors and across the campus to the student parking lot. Aron looked from side to side, well-aware that this procession of law and discipline escorting him was not going unnoticed on the campus.

When they arrived at Aron's Honda Civic, new, highly polished, two-tone brown and tan, the student quickly pulled a small canvas satchel from the trunk of his car. The satchel, stained and tarred from its life on the beach, was tied off at the top. Wordlessly, he handed the satchel to Deputy Richter.

Richter took the satchel from Aron, looked at it momentarily, seemed to heft it, before asking, Uh— Aron, you mind if I open it?"

Aron nodded, but continued to remain otherwise silent, looking alternately at Richter and the satchel he was holding. Richter waited, then said, "Uh, Aaron, I'd appreciate it if we could get you to speak up. May I open the bag? Just a simple 'yes' or 'no' will do."

"Yeah. Go ahead. You're going to anyway." Aron had adopted his earlier surly tone. And he matched it with a defiant stare first at Richer, then at Deputy Iverson.

As Richter untied the top of the satchel, Iverson stepped to his side, his notebook opened. He was scribbling notes as Richter reached inside the bag to pull out a single bungee cord. "Uh, well, there's only one in the bag," he said looking at Aron. "I thought you said there were three or four."

"Nah. That's what *you* said," Aron retorted. "What would I need with more than one or, uh...maybe two, bungee cords? What you see is what I got."

"Well, I guess for the time being, I'm going to ask Mr. Beck here to confiscate this one cord," Richter said, handing the satchel and the bungee cord back to Aron. "We have a problem that involves bungee cords. And I'm going to ask Mr. Beck to turn the cord over to the Sheriff's Department. I think for the time being we'd just better hang on to this one—and the satchel as well. Deputy Iverson will take these from Mr. Beck and sign them over to the Sheriff's Department and give you a copy of the confiscation order. That okay with you, Aron?"

Richter looked over at Mr. Beck and then toward Aron, checking closely for his reaction. He passed the satchel and bungee cord back to Aron's hands.

Aron, for his part, merely nodded. If there was some problem with this official act, he wasn't evincing any signs of his discontent. Mr. Beck walked over to Aron and took the bungee cord and satchel from his hands. These he handed over to Deputy Iverson. No words had been spoken.

XV

Alfredo sat wordless in the truck as Chris backed out of the parking space and turned his truck into the street. "I don't think that Carlos likes me very much,"Chris said, quietly. "There was just something in his manner, his tone of voice."

"No way, man...don't mind him. That's just Carlitos. Like I told you, it's his mask. Sometimes I think he doesn't really even know it happens. He comes off kind of unfriendly, but he really isn't. He doesn't take to new people very easily. Don't mind him!"

"Okay. No sweat, then." Chris smiled over at his passenger. "You want to stop off and get something to eat on the way? We can pick it up and eat as we go." He checked his rearview mirror to see Reeni following him closely.

"No. Actually, my throat's so tight that I don't think I

could swallow. I'd probably choke on Jell-O right now. But, yeah, let's stop, you got to be hungry."

"No. I can wait," Chris responded. "Maybe when I take Reeni home we'll get something. I don't know, food doesn't sound too good right now. Yeah, I guess I'm hungry, but nothing sounds even a little bit good."

The two young men drove silently for a few minutes before Chris again spoke. "Alfredo," he began, "you know we were talking about masks a little while ago? And you talked about how Mario didn't seem to have one, or need one?"

Alfredo nodded his head, looking inquisitively over at his friend.

"Well, here's something I need to say, "Chris continued. "I guess I need you to know. Aron Levin? He's not my friend. He was! But he hasn't been really since Sunday afternoon at Los Lobos when he squared off on you and Mario. I didn't know he was gonna do that; then when I saw him sucker-punch Mario yesterday. I...well, I guess he just took off his mask for good in the past couple of days. And I've just been too stupid to see what was behind the mask. It's funny. I didn't know that friends wore masks."

Alfredo stared at Chris for a moment, then smiled. "Hey. It's all right. You're not the problem here. I know that! And, anyway, we don't even know for sure just what happened...out there, last night. We'd know...if Mario could tell us..." Alfredo paused, knowing that his next words would be strangled in his throat.

They had reached the school parking lot, neither of them having paid much attention to the warm sunshine, the blooming ceonothus, the golden grasses waving gently in the afternoon breeze. The trip had been uneventful. In fact, neither remembered much of the ride back to the high school. Each was caught in his own web of thoughts.

Chris made a left turn into the parking lot and veered across the lanes to Alfredo's '66 Mustang. The traditional Wimbleton White glistened in the afternoon sun. Pulling up in the next parking slot, he looked over at Alfredo who was staring out in front of him. "He's not gonna get better," Alfredo muttered. "Dr. Jamison said as much. Did you know that? They're going to pull the plug on him." Alfredo swung around to stare at Chris. "Maybe they've already done it," he added furiously. He swung back to stare angrily out the front window of the truck.

Chris nodded. He opened his mouth to say something, but slowly closed it again. He simply didn't know what to say. He wanted desperately to say something fine, something consoling, he wanted to say that he would help Alfredo get through all of this...

Alfredo nodded. He knew. And knew that Chris couldn't help. "He didn't even know I was there.," he said quietly. "I kept saying to him 'Littlebrother, Littlebrother.' But there was nothing there. Just Mario lying on that bed, staring at nothing, just letting those machines breathe for him. Did you know that his eyes were open? He was cold. I held his hand, and it was so cold. Not like on the beach this morning...He was frigid out there. Now, he's just very cold."

Alfredo opened the car door and pulled himself out. He looked back at Chris and said, 'Thanks, buddy." Chris watched as Alfredo slid into the driver's seat of the Mustang. He shook his head slightly, started his engine, and drove away. Chris looked for and found Reeni waiting at the curb outside of the parking lot. He signaled for her to follow him, and then he too drove slowly in the direction of her house. Thoughts tore through his mind: *Why a kid like Mario? Where was the justice in all of this? Where was God last night? Apparently not at Los Lobos...*He knew that Reeni wouldn't see him crying.

 XVI

Tuesday evening was slow in its approach, but Chris and Reeni eventually pulled up outside the rectory of St. Monica's. Both youngsters sat there for a moment, before Chris looked over at Reeni, pulled her hand to his lips and kissed it softly. "Let's get this over with!" he said, smiling half-heartedly.

He stepped out of his truck and quickly moved around to open the door for Reeni. She was dressed in a smart, modestly-styled, floral-print skirt that fell in drapes to her mid-calf. Her blouse, mauve linen, was buttoned up the front and featured full, long-sleeves that buttoned at the wrist. Her make-up, as usual, was carefully and lightly applied. If she wore lipstick, it was only faintly apparent. Chris wore his uniform: pressed chinos and yellow polo shirt.

Reeni slipped out of the seat and took Chris's hand.

They both approached the front of the rectory as Father Leo opened the door to greet them. "Good!" he said. "I'm glad that you got here a little early. Maybe we can have some time to plan. Come on upstairs. We can meet in my study. We'll meet in the conference room down here when your parents arrive." With that said, Father Leo turned and led the pair of youngsters up the staircase.

Seating himself behind his desk and motioning Chris and Reeni to take the two chairs in front of his desk, Father Leo reached for his toy and began squeezing the exerciser. "Well," he said, "where should we start? Any ideas?"

Chris shifted awkwardly in his chair and took Reeni's hand, but continued to stare at the desk top in front of him. "Uh...Father, maybe we should just figure on how we are supposed to do this. I mean, how angry do you think they're going to be? We've talked about this...this afternoon. Reeni's dad's going to be pretty pissed. At least, at first. How're we gonna handle it? I'm afraid that if he gets on our case too much, I'm going to get pissed too. And I know that that's not going to help the situation at all." Chris paused and looked up at Father Leo.

"I mean, I want to protect Reeni, too. I guess that I'm asking for your help here. I would really like it if you could kind of run shot-gun for me," he continued.

Father Leo smiled. "Well...you're probably right on all accounts. Yes. From past experience—and you do understand, don't you? that this is not my first foray into this particular landscape—anyway, from past experience, we can pretty much expect *both* Mr. and Mrs. Richter to be upset! Just look for it, expect it, and, most of all, be prepared to deal with it. However," Father Leo paused before continuing, "I am going to expect you to break the news. That's definitely not something that I should do."

Chris and Reeni both flinched visibly when the doorbell rang downstairs even as they were talking. Father Leo simply smiled to them and continued. "And to answer your next question: Yes. That's why we are here. To help each other out. But, trust me: I'm not going to sit back and let anger, yours or anyone else's take over this meeting."

Mrs. Bell interrupted their discussion via the rectory's intercom. "Father Leo, the Richters and the Battlesons are here. I've put them into the conference room like you asked and told them you'd be right down."

"Fine. Thanks Mrs. Bell. I appreciate your waiting downstairs for me. I'll not be needing you again this evening. Good night. Have a peaceful sleep!" With that, Father Leo arose from his chair and looked down at the exerciser in his hand. "Well, I guess I'll not be needing *this* either," he said smiling. "Shall we go." It was not a question.

Downstairs, Father Leo opened the door to the conference room, and held it open for Reeni and Chris to pass through into the room. Both of their parents were seated at the conference table, the Battlesons in two of the three chairs on the one side, the Richters in two of the three on the other. Chris and Reeni said hello to their parents, even as both sets of parents revealed the question that was in their minds by the startled expressions on their faces.

"Chris!" Mr. Battleson said. "What're you doing here? And Reeni? I thought you guys were going to the library—we—didn't know you two were going to be here?"

Maria Richter stood as Reeni drew near her. "Sweetheart! Are you okay? We thought this was a parish meeting." Reeni, smiling shyly at her mother and shaking her head almost imperceptibly, reached over to pat her on her outstretched arm.

Father Leo, meanwhile, took a seat at the head of the conference table and motioned Chris and Reeni to take the seats to the sides of him. Chris sat next to his mother; Reeni, next to her father. "Good evening, folks," he began. "Let me start this off by thanking you for agreeing to meet here tonight."

"Excuse me, Father, but what's this all about? I'm not sure what you mean 'agreeing to meet—'" Chip Richter had straightened himself up in the oak captain's chair from his earlier, more comfortable position. "What's going on here, Reeni?" he asked, looking not at Reeni, but squarely at Chris. "What're you and Chris doing here?"

Father Leo raised his hand slightly, not enough to give offense to Mr. Richter, but enough to suggest that he wanted to continue talking. "Okay, Chip. Yes, I know that you and Maria need some explaining; so do Annie and Bob. That's why we are all here. We need to discuss some serious business. As you can probably guess." Father Leo paused, smiling at both the Richters and the Battlesons, before continuing. "So, let's begin. Chris...Reeni. You want to go on from here?"

Chris looked over at Reeni, smiling slightly, and nodded. "Yes, Father Leo. I figure it's our turn. Mom, Dad, Mr. and Mrs. Richter...well...Reeni, uh...Reeni and I are going to have...uh...a...we are going to be parents."

"What???" Chip Richter lunged out of his chair,

pushing it violently back away from the table. "What did you just say???" He stood there, his face flushed with red, his piercing eyes staring fixedly at Chris. "What have you done to my daughter???"

Maria Richter reached up and took her husband's arm. "Please, Chip. Sit down. We'll hear more. But…"

"No, Maria. No! I don't know what's going on here. Father Leo calls and asks us to a meeting. We agree. No problem. Parish stuff. We trusted him. Now we got this *problem*, this disgraceful problem. Father Leo," he continued, looking now directly at the priest. "What do *you* have to say…you were lying about this meeting from the git-go."

Richter slowly settled back into his seat as his wife continued to hold onto his arm. He looked over at his long-time friend and fellow parishioner. But Bob Battleson had slumped down into his seat, staring off into space. Meeting Chip's gaze, he quietly shook his head as if to say *don't ask me…I'm about as stunned as you are.*"

Father Leo coughed quietly. "Well, there you have it. It's not good news. Such things never are. At least not initially—"

"What the hell do you mean *initially*?" Chip Richter interrupted. "Nothing's good about this. I don't know where you're coming from. And I hope to hell you're not giving this good-for-nothing animal your blessing!"

Chris stiffened perceptibly in his chair. His dark eyes blazed momentarily with evident fury, before he lowered his head to stare at his clenched fists.

"Wait just a minute, Chip!" Bob Battleson half stood in his chair. "This is not the time to start some goddamned name calling," he retorted angrily. "Chris is not some *good-for-nothing animal* and I resent—"

Again, Father Leo slightly raised his hand. "No. We are here to discuss this problem. Please believe me. Chris and Reeni came to me because they care deeply about you all. They know they have—and this was their word—disappointed you terribly. And they asked me to help them meet with you. It's that simple—and that complex!" He looked around at each of the parents. "What could I have said over the phone?" Only Annie Battleson nodded in his direction.

"Father Leo, let me say a couple of things," Chris said, looking toward the priest. He paused before continuing. "Dad, Mom, Mr. Richter, Mrs. Richter. We both know that we have let you down. If we could take it back, we would. But we can't. We won't. Father Leo gave us our options. And there really aren't any options for us. Abortion—"

"Wait a minute, young man," Richter again began to lunge out of his seat, only to be held down by the gentle pressure of Maria Richter's hand.

"No. Please, Mr. Richter. Let me finish. I know you're pi– angry. You have a right to be. I've been dreading this meeting for several weeks now. But I know that we have to live with what we have done. And we want to live honorably and in faith. So, abortion is out. So is adoption. Reeni and I figure that if we're old enough to do what we did, we'd better face with reverence what we have to do now. And that's learn to be the best parents that we can be."

Chris paused and took a deep breath. "Mom, Dad, Mrs. and Mr, Richter. This is where we are, and we are asking your help in getting to our future. We can go it alone, but we don't want to." He looked down at his hands clasped tightly together on the table top in front of him. It was with some effort he was able to keep them from visibly trembling.

Reeni, reached across the table and placed her hand on top of his clenched fists. She smiled at him before turning in her seat to face her father. "Daddy," she began, "Chris is right. We know that we have disappointed you—all of you. We love you and would never have thought that we would be talking here with you about all this. But we are. And, Daddy, please. It's not about Chris. It's about both of us. We've talked. You know we've been serious for more than a year. You know that we wanted to get married soon…"

Chip Richter opened his mouth to speak, but Reeni, smiled shyly at him. "No, Daddy, let me finish. Yes, we weren't going to get married *this soon*. But now we are."

Reeni's father settled back in his chair. He looked over at Bob Battleson, and said, "Did you guys know about all this? Are we the only ones left in the dark?"

"No!." Annie Battleson cried out. "No, Chip, this is as much a shock to us as to you—"

"Well," Richter cut short her words, saying, "Why haven't you said anything? I mean, it seems I'm the only one upset here."

"No, Chip" Bob Battleson said, looking angrily at Richter. "No. Goddammit! Annie's correct. We're just as shocked as you are. And probably just as much in the dark. It's just that you, Chip, have been doing all the talking. We haven't had much of a chance to get a word in edgewise. Don't get me wrong," he continued, "I can understand your being upset. I *am*. And I certainly would be if Reeni were my daughter. We, probably each of us, are going to hash this out at home when we leave here. But for right now, maybe we'd better get on with what else this meeting's all about." Bob Battleson turned to Father Leo and nodded his head. "Okay, Father Leo, what now?"

Father Leo smiled at Bob Battleson. "Yes," he began, "I can surely understand your...uh, dismay, your disappointment. And, yes, that's why we are here. The bad news is out. Now, let's concentrate on the good news." He paused and stood, pushing his chair out from the table. "Here are a couple of things that you know...but that need to be said out loud. Number one," he said as he raised his right hand with his index finger raised, "Chris and Reeni are two very fine young people. Maybe among the finest. You both should be very proud parents. You've raised two really good kids.

"This does not mean we condone what has happened. And, no, Chip, to answer your question, I'm not giving Chris my blessing in the sense that you mean it. But he *and Reeni* surely have my blessing. As does the child that is surely to come." Father Leo paused to glance over at Chip and smiled. Chip Richter nodded, but did not return his smile.

Father Leo continued. Holding up his hand with two fingers extended. "Number two: Reeni and Chris want to get married as soon as possible. And I believe that we have a duty both to them and to their unborn child to encourage them to this end." He nodded toward both the Battlesons and the Richters. Annie and Maria Richter looked at each other nodding, each knowing that their roles were to be as strong sponsors of a life that Chris and

Reenie would share together.

"Wait a minute, Father," Chip Richter interjected. "I just want to say that I am—I think we all are—going to support these two. I guess I should apologize for my outbursts. It's just that—"

"No. Mr. Richter, "Chris said. "Don't apologize. I know what we've done. I couldn't imagine your *not* being pretty angry with me. I've been pretty angry with myself. But, you know that I love Reeni. We're gonna make it. I promise you.

Father Leo smiled at Chris. "Thanks, Chris. We know you do and that Reeni loves you. And this is really why we are all here. So, here's Number three, and again he raised his hand, this time with three fingers aloft. "They are going to need all the support—and love—that we can give them. However, I want you all to know that such support cannot smother…I'm saying this to all six of you. *Smothering* can destroy. And that's not what we want. In important ways, they will need to find their own way. And in just as important ways, they will need to know that you will be there for them."

Father Leo looked over at Reeni and then at Chris. "Chris, it's your turn. I know that you and Reeni have discussed your immediate future. Let's hear from you."

"Well, Mom, Dad. I'm pretty much aware that you expected me to go on to college. I will. But right now, as soon as I graduate, I'm getting a full-time job. Maybe, I can get a couple of college courses—some of the EMT and fire-fighting ones out of the way at night. Reeni's going to start her nursing program as soon as she can after the baby is born, just as we had planned. We figure that between the two of us, we can take care of the baby—but we might need a baby-sitter every now and then. We think that we'll be able to handle it. But not alone!" Chris looked over at his mother and smiled quietly. Annie Battleson returned his smiled with a warm one of her own.

Reeni stood up and moved to stand next to Chris. "I just want you all to know that what Chris is saying about our future plans is stuff that we have talked out. He's not just talking for himself. He's talking for both of us." She looked over at her father and smiled. "It's going to be okay, Daddy. I know it is."

Chip Richter smiled, but it was a sad smile. "Well, I guess that there's not much I can say or do at this point. Except to say that yes...you both *are right*, I am disappointed. It isn't how I expected to see the two of you complete your high school. I guess I will get over my disappointment, but, well..."His voice trailed off leaving the impact of words to fill the silence that followed.

Father Leo again coughed and spoke. "No, it would be silly of me to suggest that there isn't disappointment among all six of you. I'd be shocked, myself, if one of you wasn't, uh...looking at the future with some uncertainty. However, I think that with our faith in God, our love of each other, our *need* for each of us to care for each other, we can get over the immediacy of our feelings tonight. We can, we must, go forward in the firm knowledge that we have the care and *the love* of an infant to sustain us.

He halted briefly to look at each of his visitors. "Chris," he asked, "is there anything more that you want to say this evening?"

"No, Father, I guess not. Unless our parents...uh...well, unless they have some questions..."

Father Leo looked around him. The parents, in turn, shook their heads. Chip Richter, the last to shake his head, looked at both Chris and Reeni, saying, "Yeah, there are a thousand questions that I have, and I suspect that neither of you has an answer to any one of them." He smiled for the first time since Reeni and Chris had entered the conference room. "I guess that I just want you to know that I was upset tonight, I still am. But I know that tomorrow it'll be somewhat better for me. And the next day. Chris, I've known you a long time. I know you're not what I called you – and I truly apologize for my language. From this moment on, I guess you're going to be my son-in-law. So start thinking…starting tomorrow, you could call me *Dad* or call me *Chip*. The choice is yours." With that, Chip Richter pushed himself back from the table and stood to shake hands with Chris. He then took Reeni in his arms and hugged her tightly. Maria followed, taking first Chris into her arms, and then clasping Reeni to herself as well.

Bob and Annie Battleson met the two youngsters from around the other side of the table. Both parents embraced the two; Annie smiled up at Reeni, saying, "Welcome to our lives, daughter!"

XVII

Life in the ICU waiting room, the hallway, the doctors' lounge, had not changed much over the past several hours. Alfredo had returned to the hospital after having gone home to change clothes. He had taken off the sweatshirt that Chris had loaned him in the morning and tossed it in the laundry hamper, put on clean poplin slacks and a blue, short-sleeve, button-down dress shirt, had changed from his sneakers to a pair of loafers, all the time wondering to himself, *Why am I doing this? Who is really gonna give a shit what I look like?* Still he did change into what he guessed was acceptable attire, shuffled, purposefully slowly downstairs, slid into the seat of his Mustang, and started the engine.

He drove just as slowly back to the hospital, thinking one of two things: *Mario was still alive, but on the machines* or *they've pulled the plug on my Littlebrother.* He knew that facing either option was probably going to take all of the emotional strength he could muster. On the trip downtown he had tried several times to reach his parents, but they weren't answering their cell phones. "Probably just well," he muttered aloud.

Entering the hospital reception area, he checked in at the desk. The nurse told him that "Mario Alhambra is in the ICU. The nurses up there will direct you." He was expected. She gave him directions which Alfredo realized, as he faced the labyrinthine corridors of the hospital, that he had hardly heard. Still he followed the main corridor until he confronted a nurse who gave him additional directions.

Alfredo took the elevator to the second floor and walked the long corridor leading to the ICU, when Carlos stepped into the hall behind him calling to him, "Alfredo, we're in here!"

He spun around to face his cousin. "Carlitos! Jesus, am I glad it's you. How are Mom and Daddy doing? Are they in there? How's Mario? Where is he? They still got him on life-support? How long–"

"Hold on, honcho," Carlos grabbed Alfredo by the shoulders. "Which question you want me to answer first?" He smiled at his cousin. "Fredo. Slow down! Just come on in here. We'll talk. I'll fill you in on everything. No. Your mom and dad are in with Mario, so is Father Miguel – they've been in there the last hour or so."

Carlos led Mario into the ICU visitors' lounge, empty now of other visitors. Alfredo dropped into a steel and orange leatherette chair and stretched his legs out in front of him. "Okay. I'll just sit and listen, but dang, Carlitos, I'm glad to see you. Things're not so good right now—

especially when I'm alone to just think bad thoughts. So, what's been happening?"

Carlos pulled a similar steel and green leatherette chair up in front of his cousin and sat down. He took a couple of deep breaths. "This is gonna be tough, Fredo. But here goes. They moved Mario up here just about the time that you left here with that guy, Chris. We all came up here. I went in to see Mario...Then Uncle Ricardo and Aunt Elena came in. We just kinda stood around talking to each other and to Mario. He wasn't doing much in the way of paying attention!" Carlos smiled at his cousin, but Alfredo couldn't bring himself to return the smile. Instead, his eyes began to tear over for the umpteenth time since early this morning.

"Yeah. I know it's not funny. I didn't mean to be flip, Okay, Fredo?" He moved to wrap his arm around Alfredo's shoulders, hugging him briefly before releasing him.

"No. I know, Carlitos. It's okay. I'm just still having problems, I guess. I'm gonna get hold of myself...I promise!"

"Okay. So, then this doctor, Jamison comes in, and he talks about – well, actually, he pretty much gave them the alternatives–"

"Which are?" Alfredo interrupted.

"Hey, man...would you give me a chance!" Carlos lightly tapped his cousin across the cheek. "So Jamison basically says *A*...we could keep on the life-support system...or *B*...we could shut down the machines and see if Mario's gonna make it on his own. Apparently, they don't really know...But I think they do. Jamison keeps throwing out the problem of...well, what he calls 'an oxygen-starved brain.'"

Carlos hesitated for a moment. "Alfredo…they're still in there. With Mario. Holding his hands, talking to him. You want to know what I think?"

Alfredo reached across and took Carlos' hand. He gripped it tightly. "Yeah. I guess I do. I guess I need someone to think for me. What do you think?"

"They gotta let the kid go. I think he's gone, Fredo. Mario left us a while ago. He's not there anymore. And he wouldn't want us here waiting beside something that *was* Mario!"

Alfredo kept his grip on Carlos' hand, but dropped his head to his chest. His shoulders were visibly shaking. "That's my brother we're talking about, Carlitos. That's Littlebrother…"

"Hey Fredo," Carlos whispered to him, drawing his face mere inches from Alfredo's. "I know. I know. But Mario's gone – and gone to a better place…at least that's what we've got to believe. And I do believe. Now, it's up to us to come to grips with what is. You have to, because you have to help Aunt Elena and Uncle Ricardo. They're the ones who have got to let go too!"

Alfredo began nodding his head. He understood, but he didn't want to. He wanted things to be the way they were…even as he knew that things had changed irrevocably.

"Father Miguel came in here a little while ago. He's in there with your parents. I guess we just have to wait…" Carlos stood up, wanting very much to take Alfredo into his arms as he had done countless times when Alfredo was just a little kid and Carlos was the role-model teenager – big, strong, protective.

114

Suddenly the door to the lounge opened briskly. Ricardo Alhambra stood there a moment, breathing heavily. "Alfredo! You're here! Good. You and Carlitos should come in here. We've decided to let Mario make it on his own. You should probably see him for a minute before the doctors...uh, remove the machines."

Alfredo looked over at his father questioningly. He started to speak, but found he had no words for what he wanted to ask.

His father simply shook his head. "We don't know. Dr. Jamison says that it's pretty much up to Mario now. Either he makes it or he doesn't. What he's really afraid of is that Mario still isn't getting oxygen to his brain...which means that even if he can make it on his own, well..." Mr. Alhambra again shook his head. "It's too difficult to say, Fredo. Just come on in here and tell him that you love him. I want to believe that he'll hear you. Can you do that, Fredo?"

He turned then abruptly and walked back into the ICU's cubicle where Mario lay. Alfredo followed his father, with Carlos tailing closely. Alfredo's dad moved to stand against the wall, shoulder to shoulder with Father Miguel. Both young men, nodding solemnly to Father Miguel, walked slowly up to Mario's bedside. Elena Alhambra moved quietly to stand beside her son. "He's not responding to much," she whispered to Alfredo, "but just take his hand, Freddie. Maybe, he'll know..." Her voice trailed off as Alfredo grasped Mario's unresponsive hand.

Alfredo stared at his little brother's inert form. The sheet had been drawn up to his neck, with his arms and hands lying outside of the covers at his side. The IVs were still attached; a breathing apparatus had been affixed to his nose. His head had been shaved across the front brow. The slashing blow he had received at the hands of Aron Levin was a yellowish purple stain across the side of his temple.

"Hey, Littlebrother," he said grasping hold of Mario's hand. "How're you doing? We're here to help you get better." Alfredo paused and looked over at his father. Mr. Alhambra merely nodded his head. "Please, Mario, you gotta help yourself." Alfredo dropped his head to his chest. Tears began to cloud his eyesight. "It's not fair, Ma. It's just not fair! Why can't we help him?"

Dr. Jamison had quietly entered the cubicle even as Alfredo was speaking. Ricardo Alhambra looked over at his wife who nodded to him. She took Alfredo by the arm and turned him back to Carlos who stood waiting glumly behind his cousin. "Why don't you two go back and wait in the lounge for a while. This is something that your Daddy and I have to deal with. Just go back in there and say a couple of prayers – for Mariolito, yes! But for your Daddy and me as well."

Alfredo and Carlos backed out of the cubicle and entered the still empty lounge; they took their seats. Alfredo leaned back in his chair and stared silently off into space. Carlos pushing his chair back away from the near proximity that he had held earlier, sighed. "You know, Fredo, maybe it's all for the best. Like I said, Mario's already better off, he's already in a better place. We gotta just leave it like that! You understand?"

Alfredo slowly focused on his cousin. "Yeah. Carlitos, I know, I know. I guess it's all been said and done."

Carlos quietly shook his head. He paused momentarily

watching as Alfredo regained some composure. "Tell me, Alfredo," he said changing the subject. "You seem pretty tight all of a sudden with this guy, Chris...whatever his last name is. Oh yeah. Battleson. You sure he's okay?"

Alfredo got up from his chair and walked to the door leading into the ICU. "Sure," he said, his back to Carlos. I don't know about 'tight.' But today, this morning, he was pretty much on top of things. I told him, I didn't know how I'd have handled the mess this morning without him there. He...well...he was *there*. So yeah, he's all right. Why?"

"Well, Fredo, from what we've discovered, he was last seen as a pretty good friend of this asshole, Aron Levin. That's all. I just want to make sure I know where he stands in all of this."

"No. We've been through that pretty much, Alfredo smiled faintly as he turned to Carlos. "He's pretty—no, he's very pissed—by what Aron did and, like Chris says, what he hadn't seen in the guy. No. Chris is okay."

"Good. No problem, then," Carlos answered, but looked across the room and away from Alfredo's gaze.

XVIII

Chris and Reeni left the rectory of St. Monica's with their parents in tow. They all had bade Father Leo goodbye in his study. He did not follow them down the stairs and out the front door, for the priest knew better than to intercede in their leave-taking. The parting had been considerably more friendly than Chris had expected. He was glad that Mr. Richter had offered to shake hands. That single moment relieved some of the stress that had been building in his body all evening. Yet he found, as he walked down the front walkway, that he ached all over. *Must be I'm stressed out from the whole meeting,* he thought to himself.

Reeni took his hand in hers as they walked toward the street. She paused at the sidewalk, looking up at Chris. "I'm going to ride home with Mom and Dad, Chris. I know that that's what they want. And tonight, I really need for them to know that I am still their little girl. Do you mind?"

"No. Of course not. It's something you need to do. I just hope your dad is okay. Maybe talking to you will soften him even more. But could you tell your dad how much I appreciated the hand-shake. Would you do that for me?"

"Sure!" And she leaned toward Chris to give him a quick kiss goodnight, before heading toward her parents' car.

Chris turned to find his parents waiting for him. "Look," he said, "you guys mind if I just take a quiet ride all by my lonesome? I'll be home early. We can talk. But I think I just need some time to straighten out my head — and ease my body. I'm think I'm pretty well strung-out right now!" He paused before adding somewhat as an afterthought, "And I'll fill you in on the way my morning went, too. I guess I really haven't seen enough of you today…"

Both Bob Battleson and Annie looked searchingly at their son. Chris's father spoke first. "No. Sure. Take a quick ride. But, son, please don't be late. We do need to talk—and tonight's as good a night as any, I think."

Annie Battleson looked closely at her son a second time, "You're going to be okay?" It was a question, not a statement.

Chris hugged her tightly, saying, "Yeah. I'm fine. I just need to unwind a little. I'll be home in an hour, hour and a half at most." He smiled at both of them, and turned to get in his truck. He halted suddenly, and looked back at them. They were both still standing there, curbside, staring after him. He smiled again and said, "Thanks, you guys. Tonight was pretty rough, I know. But thanks for being my parents!" With that, he slid into the driver's seat, started the engine, and drove off, honking lightly as he did so.

At the first boulevard stop, he fished his cell phone from the glove compartment and dialed a number. It rang several times before Alfredo answered.

"Yeah?"

"Hey, Alfredo, this is Chris. How are you doing? You still at the hospital?"

Alfredo paused for a moment before replying. "Chris. Yes. We're still here. Thanks for calling."

"So," Chris replied, "How's Mario? Getting better, I hope!"

"No. Actually, they took him off life-support about thirty minutes ago…" Alfredo paused so long that Chris thought they had been disconnected.

"Hey, Alfredo…you there…?"

"Yeah, Chris, I'm here. Sorry. I just had to stop for a minute. Anyway…Mario lasted about three minutes off the machines. Then, well…he just quit breathing. Kind of just like the doctors said…So, that's about the size of things."

"Shit! Fredo. I'm really sorry. Truly." It was Chris's turn to pause. "How're you doing, man," he said at last.

"Well…I guess I'd better learn to live my life without a little brother. It sucks, Chris, it sucks big-time."

There was again a lengthy pause, before Chris finally spoke. "Listen, Fredo. I'm on my way to Los Lobos. I need some time to get away from things. I figure we both do. How 'bout I stop by the hospital and pick you up. You could just ride along. I won't need to make conversation.

Just a ride out of this mess for a while. Whatta you say?"

"Yeah, that sounds good," Alfredo said, "but maybe I better stay on here with my folks. They're pretty well done in by all this, too. But thanks—Chris, hold on a minute, okay?" Alfredo's end of the conversation went silent. Chris waited, wondering what the interruption was all about. Then suddenly, Alfredo spoke again.

"Hey, Chris. Yeah. Pick me up. Carlitos says for me to 'get the hell outta here.' He says he can take care of things for a while. So yeah. I'll be waiting out in front. Okay?"

"I'm on my way, dude. I'll be there in maybe six or seven minutes." Chris' finger shut off the call and pulled a u-turn to head back toward the hospital.

XIX

Chris picked Alfredo up at the entrance to the hospital moments later; he climbed into the passenger side of the truck, nodding to Chris as he did so. "Thanks!" he murmured as much to himself as to Chris.

"Not a problem, Fredo. We're both due for a little quiet time—as they used to tell us in first grade." He paused before continuing. "Tell you what: you want to talk, talk. You want to just shut up and ride in silence, I can handle that too. Okay?"

"Yeah. That's fine by me. And to tell you the truth...I don't know what I want. Well, that's not true. I want Littlebrother back. I think I'm dealing with a world that I experienced before I learned to read, maybe even before I learned to speak...Everything seems to be in pictures – gray pictures, black pictures, white pictures. I'm having trouble understanding a world without Mariolito...Jesus,

I'm fucking crying again! Just drive, Chris! This has got to stop!"

Chris drove out of the downtown area and turned right onto the Los Lobos Road. He slowed considerably as a car pulled off a side road and turned onto Los Lobos Road, heading in the opposite direction toward town.

Alfredo watched the car for a moment, then commented, "That's my Uncle John and Aunt Rita, Carlito's mom and dad. They're probably heading up to see Ma and Daddy. That's their ranch back there – well, along here. Uncle John manages the walnut and almond groves out here."

"That right?" Chris answered. "Dang, I mean I pass these orchards all the time and I guess I never really thought about it. All these trees? I figured they just grew by themselves!"

"No. Actually, they take quite a bit of work." Alfredo laughed softly. "Uncle John is pretty much busy all year round, a lot of irrigation, lot of weed-control, pruning…but especially in the late summer and early fall when the crop gets ripe. Carlitos, he works here full time. He helps with the orchards, of course, but he mostly manages the cattle ranch. That's our property on the other side of the road, too." Alfredo paused to point to the cattle that were grazing across a vast landscape of grasses and rolling hills.

"*Your* property? You *own* this?" Chris asked incredulously. "You guys own all of this?"

"Well…yes." Alfredo said quietly. The land's been in the Alhambra-Alvarez family a long, long time. There was this deal in the original deed that has been there ever since: the property cannot be sold outside of the family.

And it sure as hell cannot be subdivided by some get-rich-quick land developer! We're not much interested in cementing over the ag land!" He laughed. "I've been working summers on the ranch ever since I was a kid. That's pretty much why Carlitos and I are so close, I guess. We've been working together every summer for a long time. That, and, of course, he's kind of my big brother."

It was Chris's turn to stare out the side windows, to the groves on the left, to the cattle on the right. "Must be a lot of acres,"he said.

"Yep. 'Bout nineteen hundred, counting all the outbuildings. Takes a lot of work. Last summer, we painted just about every friggin' barn, shed, outhouse, whatever, on the place. But, it's cool too," Alfredo added. "You do your thing. You work at your own pace. You get to be outdoors. But you gotta get the work done too. Carlitos can be a slave-driver when he thinks things are not going according to his plan!"

"You say that you guys have had this property for generations?" Chris asked.

"Yeah…it comes down from my great-great grandfather. It's a weird story. You might be shocked. Not too many people know the ins and outs of it. You game?" Alfredo looked over at Chris, smiling broadly.

"Go for it. Try and shock me!" Chris said, returning Alfredo's smile.

"Okay. Here goes, but I'll make it short. You know this valley's called Dos Padres Valley. Right? You know why?"

"Yeah. Sure. Every kid in the valley gets a history lesson in it. Sister Consuelo. Third grade. 'Two Padres.'

Right?" Chris didn't wait for an answer; he just continued his history lesson. "The two missionary fathers who founded the mission – along with Serra, of course – they're the ones who set up the Dos Padres Station that started everything here. I even remember their names...Father Miguel and Father Juan Carlos."

"Well, yes, but that's about it as far as your history lesson tells it. All the Sister Consuelos always, uh...should I say *omit* a couple of significant details. You first should know that my great-great grandfather was one of those padres; he was—

"Whoa, Fredo. Just back up a second." Chris looked over at Alfredo, laughing as he did so. You can't be a grandfather, or whatever, and a padre too."

"Uh...you got that wrong, Chris," Alfredo laughed even harder. "Wrong *verb*. Not *can't—shouldn't*. And you keep making me laugh, and we're gonna have to stop to let me take a piss."

"Okay. So your grandfather—no, your great-great grandfather...what?"

"Well, in the language of my family—my father, who thinks the whole story is pretty funny—anyway in our language, my "great-great grandfather knocked-up an Indian maiden...just like they sing in the song."

"Shee—it!" Chris exclaimed. "And all this time, I thought they were the saintly padres who founded our little burg. Wow! Those nuns didn't tell half the story, did they!"

"Nope!" Alfredo laughed again. But here's the good news. When they found out, and actually, he—the *sainted padre*, as you say, really loved the Mission Indian girl, well, when they found out, they kicked him out of the

Franciscan order, set him up as the sole proprietor of the Dos Padres Station, and because they didn't think that it would amount to much deeded him all this land. So to make a complicated story short, the land is deeded down through the Alhambra-Alvarez family.

Chris drove along, nodding his head, processing this newer version of Dos Padres Valley. Alfredo paused momentarily, before continuing. "I think, so does Daddy, that it was kind of like hush money—you don't ever admit you were a padre and you can keep the land. Daddy and Uncle John are the heirs. Maybe...well, no, Carlitos and I are too; we'll get it eventually."

They both had been throwing off tension so easily that neither realized how little time the trip to Los Lobos had taken. Chris pulled into the parking lot, deliberately avoiding parking anywhere near the spot he had parked earlier this morning. Each young man sat back in his seat, staring out at the waves breaking whitely in the moonlight. The fog that hung on the horizon had not yet begun its slow creep landward. The night air, still warm from the reflecting heat of the sands, had not given over to the usual off-shore winds. The night sky was clear, starlit, softly black. Even the waves added to the quiet by gently rolling over on themselves with only a murmur of lapping waters.

Chris shifted in his seat and opened the door of his Toyota. He bent down and kicked off his loafers and peeled off his socks. "I'm going to take a walk. I love this time of night here." He slipped out of the truck, shoved his shoes and socks in onto the floorboard, and looked over at Alfredo.

Alfredo, still staring straight ahead, replied, "Yeah.

This is okay. Maybe I'll follow in a minute or two. Just sitting here like this is doing good things to my mind." Chris quietly shut the door and disappeared behind the truck. Alfredo, turning around in his seat, could see Chris changing into a pair of beach shorts.

He watched as Chris, kicking sand up in front on him, trudged along the low dune toward the surf. *Jesus, Mario,* he thought. *How am I gonna handle this. Each day, each morning? Tonight's a good beginning. Maybe I can remember tonight tomorrow and the next day...*

Moments later, Alfredo followed Chris' example. Shedding his loafers and socks, he rolled his pant legs up to his knees, and followed Chris' path down to the shoreline. He could see Chris some twenty yards farther down the beach, wading ankle-deep in the rising tide. *Was it this beautiful last night, Mario?* he asked. And then, in answer, he remembered, *No, the fog came in early on a brisk off-shore breeze. Last night was spring-time-chill in Dos Padres Valley. Shit! This has been some twenty-four fucking long hours!"*

"Hey," he called out to Chris. "Wait up." Alfredo picked up the pace and jogged down the shoreline, now and then kicking up water as he ran. He saw Chris pull his polo shirt over his head and toss it above the line of the tide; he watched as Chris turned and splashed into the cold surf. And even as Alfredo came up parallel to him, Chris lightly dove into the small wave that lapped at his waist.

Chris surfaced spitting water as he did so. "Come on in!" he shouted back at Alfredo. "It'll do you more good than you can believe. Just do it!"

Alfredo paused. He looked down at his trousers,

already wet at his knees. Slowly he unbuttoned his shirt, thinking *this is insane!* He too tossed his shirt above the tide line, looked momentarily down at his dress pants and dropped them to his ankles. Stepping out of the pants, he wondered, *Why the hell did I put these clothes on anyway. I knew it was stupid when I was doing it.*

Alfredo, in his boxers, walked to the edge of the surf and watched as Chris once again dove into an on-coming wave, surfaced, and swam farther seaward. He then stepped lightly into the surf, splashing water until he, too, stood in waist-deep surf. Diving into the next wave, he quickly swam out to where Chris floated beyond the surf. Chris was shooting water skyward and laughing as he did so.

"This is great. There's nobody here to screw with us, to mess with our minds. Just you and me and this goddamned fine ocean!" he shouted to Alfredo. And Alfredo, treading water, laughed openly with Chris, acknowledging the wonder of it all…the soft darkness, the quiet power of the ocean moving beneath him, the gentle pull of peace emanating from the starry night.

They swam for a few minutes more before both turned toward the shore. And, as Chris looked over at Alfredo, he knew…it was a race. Alfredo was laughing at him. And he had the advantage. He'd already started toward shore. So Chris dug in and began his plowing his way through the salty water. Alfredo was sitting in the shallows along the shore-line when Chris stood up in the knee-deep water. He was laughing. "I really did just pee in my pants!" he snorted.

Back at the truck, Chris pulled two towels from behind his seat, tossing one to Alfredo. "Just so you know, you gotta dry off *outside* my vehicle. Nobody wet sits on my seats," he laughed.

Alfredo, laughing too, said, "Just how much shit do you keep stashed behind your seat there?"

The drive back began uneventfully. Then, Alfredo, still drying his hair, said, "Chris...Thanks. I needed this. An hour ago I didn't think I'd be feeling this way ever again. The cold, the water, the swim, everything...it just took every ugly...oh, well, whatever! I don't know what the hell I'm talking about. I just know that I feel clean again."

Hey, don't thank me! I needed it too. When I picked you up tonight, I was ready to pop the first guy that got in my face. And I'd probably just continue to bloody the jerk up until I got all the shit outta my system!" Chris said grimly.

"Whoa. Man. What're you talking about?" Alfredo asked, glancing over at Chris's suddenly bleak expression.

"Actually, Fredo...today, no, tonight has been weird. Did you know – no, you probably wouldn't have had any way of knowing—anyway, you know Reeni and I have been dating for awhile?"

Alfredo nodded. "Yeah, I've seen you guys together. She was with you in the bathroom with Mario yesterday."

"Yes. Well, Reeni's pregnant," Chris said. "And tonight was the night that we *got* to tell our parents. The good news is that we had Father Leo on our side. The bad news is Reeni's father was pretty pissed off. He even called me a *good-for-nothing animal*. At least that's what I remember! But, what I mean to say is that the whole thing ended pretty positively...at least, I think it did. But it sure as hell took its toll on my body. I was so tightly wound up when the meeting was finally over...I couldn't believe it."

"Jesus, Chris," Alfredo muttered. "I guess I really do owe you one more time. I didn't know you had *that* to look forward to tonight! Shit!"

"Well, actually, I pretty much forgot all about the meeting for a while this morning. I didn't really even remember until I picked Reeni up this afternoon. So, no sweat!"

Afredo paused. "Uh, I gotta ask you a question? It's kind of personal...How do you all feel about this? I mean about having a baby? That's pretty scary." Alfredo looked questioningly over at Chris.

"Oh, I think that both Reeni and I are okay with the situation, now. Yeah. You're right, it's kind of scary. But I guess that we've had awhile to get used to the idea...you know? And we have plans...We're going to do it!" Chris smiled over at Alfredo. "We can handle this...Shit, I figure if I can just get through dealing with her dad, I can handle anything!"

Alfredo laughed suddenly out loud. "Hey. You mind a joke?"

Chris looked over at him laughing as well. "No. . what're you thinking?"

Staring straight ahead, but still laughing, Alfredo asked, "Maybe you should name the kid Juan-Miguel — you know...in memory of our sainted padres!"

"No way, dude! Jesus, can you just hear Reeni's dad! He'd friggin' blow my head off!" But Chris continued to laugh out loud for several more minutes.

Again, as their conversation floated through the truck's interior, the drive back into town passed quickly. Chris looked over at Alfredo, "Where do you want me to drop you—home or the hospital?"

"Hospital. That's where my 'stang's parked." Alfredo said. "I guess I'll drive on home from there. I don't know where Ma and Daddy are."

"You got it, dude. You just take care and we'll talk tomorrow!" Chris said, pulling into the hospital parking lot.

"Hey. I almost forgot. The Rosary for Mario is tomorrow night at the Mission. 7:30. I'd like it if you could make it!" Alfredo slid out of the Toyota, and looked back at Chris. "Can you do it?"

"We'll be there, me and Reeni. Later!" Chris called, pulling away from the curb.

XX

When Sam Beck arrived at his desk Wednesday morning, a message was already waiting for him: *Please return Mr. Levin's call ASAP.* Beck's secretary added, as she mentioned the phone call, that Mr. Levin had peremptorily declined to state "the nature of his call."

Beck waited until classes had begun that morning to return the call. Having been called at his home last night and informed of the death of Mario Alhambra, he was in no mood to speak to Mr. Levin. The death of any student left a terrible and gaping hole in the fabric of a high school. He knew from experience that the news of Mario's death would be flying across the campus even as he sat there. He might be needed on campus today of all days during the opening of the school day; he also wanted to check that Aron Levin was properly in place in the on-campus suspension classroom, for Aron Levin was as much in his mind as was the death of that good child who had been sitting in his office just two days ago.

A simple call to the Detention Center was all that was necessary. He discovered that Aron was absent from school this day. The information gave Beck some food for thought, food that fed his brain even as he punched in the telephone number his secretary had provided him as he heard the bell for first period ring in the hallway outside of his office. His call was answered immediately by a Levin secretary who performed the usual monitoring strategy of who's calling and why...

When Beck gave her his name and suggested that he was returning Mr. Levin's call, she asked him to hold and within a matter of seconds put him through. Beck again identified himself, saying, "Mr. Levin, this is Sam Beck from Mission High School. I have a message here on my desk that you called earlier this morning."

"Yes. To get right down to it," Mr. Levin snapped, "I believe that you need to know that Aron and I have discussed the matter of his suspension Monday afternoon, as well as his day in your so-called in-school suspension—at some length, actually. I have decided that Aron will be better served working off his suspension at our home. Not all of his teachers provided him with work, yesterday. It seems pointless his spinning his wheels in a classroom full of *deadbeats*. Additionally, I'm not convinced that you have dealt fairly with Aron. His side of the story suggests a considerably less serious action than you indicated to me over the phone."

"I see,"Beck answered. "Well, since I'm not privy to Aron's side of the problem as recounted to you, I guess I cannot comment on—"

"Well," Levin cut short Beck's words. "I can tell you

Aron's side and will expect you to take his words into account in changing your decision about Aron's suspension *and* his Saturday detentions, as well. Additionally, I also highly resent your calling in the Sheriff's Department."

"Uh, Mr. Levin. I would appreciate your not interrupting me." Beck said softly. "This is not a courtroom, and I am most assuredly not on trial here. What I do know, however, is that Aron's suspension stands, as does the place he will serve his suspension – *on this campus*. Now, if you choose to keep him home, we can only assume that you do so because he is ill. Otherwise, these absences will be accounted as unexcused. Which, of course, will set in motion a whole *other* series of circumstances," Beck concluded.

"Well, that is, indeed, unfortunate. I rather assumed that we could come to some more equitable conclusion regarding your actions against my son." Levin's words were as uncompromising as his tone. And he paused, waiting for Beck to answer.

"Ummm. Yes, well. I do understand your concern for Aron's welfare, and, while you may not concur with our decisions, I do applaud your standing up for your son. However, you also must understand that Aron did not deny the sucker-punch or the ugly language he used. And it was for those actions that Aron was suspended— however he may have related the incident to you. And—"

Again, Levin interrupted, saying, "Yes, but it would seem that Aron was provoked...that this young punk, what's his name, Mario, initiated the encounter."

And, again, Beck suggested that he be allowed to finish his part of the conversation. "Mr. Levin, I would appreciate being allowed to answer your concerns. Which is to say beyond Aron's actions...no, we did not call in the Sheriff's Department. The two deputies came to us and asked to have Aron called out of his in-class suspension. We merely complied, as you well know we should, with their request. I am still in the dark as to exactly why they did so."

"That," Levin said evenly, "is not Aron's take on your actions. He feels, as I must agree, that Mission High School, you in particular, are out to get him." Again, Levin, paused, waiting for a response from Beck.

"I suspect, Mr. Levin," Beck answered after pausing himself, "that there is not much I can say which might convince you otherwise. We, of course, have well-established policies on the campus for dealing with troubling situations. And these are policies that are spelled out in detail in our *Student Handbook*. We follow these policies in dealing with such problems as those that Aron apparently brought on himself."

"Fine," Levin retorted. "I'll deal with the Sheriff's Department this morning. And I will deal with Mario and his family. I expect to get to the bottom of this 'problem' as you so-call it. Before we leave off this discussion could you please share with me this Mario kid's last name."

"Uh...yes, I guess I could. However, I think there is something that you ought to know." Beck again paused quickly assessing just what words he would use. "I got word late last night that Mario died. He was admitted yesterday morning to the hospital and died in the ICU. He had been, apparently, brutally attacked Monday evening. I really don't have much more information at this point...Other than, of course, these facts. But, yes. His name is...uh, was Mario Alhambra. Now. Is there anything else I can help you with at this point?"

"No." Mr. Levin paused momentarily before he asked, "He died, did you say? Well, that does provide us with a new wrinkle. Is this Mario Alhambra somehow related to our City Manager, Richard Alhambra?"

"As a matter of fact, yes, Mr. Levin, I believe he is. Mario is Mr. Alhambra's son," Beck replied.

"I see. Well, I will not thank you for your cooperation. But I do suspect that we will speak again." With that, Levin abruptly disconnected. And Beck sat there with the receiver gripped in his hand wondering just what Levin meant *by getting to the bottom of this problem.*

XXI

Aron Levin, this Wednesday afternoon, was basking in the warm spring weather, polishing his freshly painted, newly-washed Honda Civic. Its brown and tan sheen glistened in the bright sunlight. The temperature, this day, had risen to almost 78 degrees. Aron, having moved his two-door convertible to the shade of a small stand of birch trees along the driveway, was deliberately making a statement. He had put on a pair of beach shorts, tossed his shirt onto the front porch, and padded barefoot around his car, applying wax, polishing, applying another coat of wax. His car stereo was running through a new CD collection of rap. Aron was very happy.

This'll teach that son-of-a-bitch, Beck, he thought, smiling to himself. *He's gonna rue the day he went up against Dad. That asshole doesn't stand a chance against my dad. He doesn't know shit about what a lawyer can do to you!* He moved into the sunlight to catch a couple of rays while the wax on a portion of the hood dried to a white sheen. Then, after applying a coat of wax to a new area of the hood, he rubbed vigorously the dried, whited wax to bring the metal to a fine glisten, before applying another coat. It was a satisfying piece of work. Bringing the car to a new shine was gratifying. Being out here, doing what he was doing, dressed as if he'd not a care in the world—well. that was pretty gratifying as well. *All those deadbeat jerks sitting stupidly in the suspension classroom were...well, just that, deadbeat jerks. Too bad Beck can't seem me now...catching a few rays, working on my car!* He was so wrapped up in his efforts on the Honda and in his thoughts that he didn't hear Buddy and Geoff drive up to the curb until Geoff honked his horn.

"How's the suspension going, Aron?" Geoff called. "I see you're busy doing the schoolwork that you brought home!"

"Screw that noise," Aron called back genially. "I'm just working my way through my punishment – and enjoying every minute of it! You guys gonna get out of the car and get over here and help me, or what? I got a lot of work to get my wheels here up to snuff!"

Both Geoff and Buddy climbed out of the car. Geoff in the lead. The pair of them were a picture of opposites. Geoff, tall and wiry, moved with the kind of grace that most athletes possess without even knowing they do so; his surfer's tan lent him the healthy appearance of a self-assured lifestyle. His Levis had been ironed carefully so that the crease down the center of the pant legs contrasted sharply with the fact that they were, indeed,

Levis. His polo shirt, too, looked immaculately pressed, as if it had just come off the rack at Robinsons/May.

Buddy, although equally tanned from his hours at Los Lobos, was the typical high school kid who hadn't quite begun the maturing process that many of his age begin late in their teens. It was a fact that he was acutely conscious of. His two surfing pals, Aron and Geoff, looked ready to board the train to life "after high school"; Buddy looked as if he wasn't exactly sure just where the train station was! Thus it was that both Geoff and Aron seemed to make all the decisions; Buddy mostly tagged along, glad to be their friend.

"So what's happening? How come you didn't show up to school today?" Geoff said, walking up to slug Aron on the shoulder. "Too bad you're having *such trouble* dealing with this suspension crap!"

Aron turned toward Geoff, smiling broadly. "My dad's handling that asshole Beck. Dad told me I didn't have to serve the detention at school, that they couldn't make me. He told me it was okay to stay home, do my detention-bit right here. Dad's gonna handle Beck big time! And he's gonna deal with the Sheriff about those two asshole deputies that were on my case."

Aron turned back to the hood of his car and the white sheen that he was attacking. "So what's happening at school? Any news?" He turned to glance at Buddy, saying, "Hey, Buddy-boy, what's happening? You don't look so good. You okay?"

"No. Things aren't looking so good," Buddy mumbled. "Did you know that that Mario Alhambra-kid died last night? The story is he never regained consciousness from when those two guys picked him up on the beach." Buddy's words were barely above a whisper. His voice quavered as he spoke.

"Yeah," Geoff continued. "That's really weird. What the hell was he doing at Los Lobos all night?"

"Golly-gee," Aron countered, sarcastically. "You got me!" And he turned from polishing the Honda to stare intently at Buddy. "What's your problem, Buddy?"

"Aron...I'm scared. Scareder than I have ever been. We're in real trouble. What if they find out?" Buddy said. He was trembling visibly.

"Forget it, Buddy. Nobody's gonna find out anything. We're free and clear – that is if you don't blow the whole thing. You just make sure that you shut your fucking mouth. Starting now!" As Aron spat these words of warning at Buddy, he had moved to stand directly in front of him. He used his index finger to poke Buddy in the chest as if to punctuate his words.

"What the hell's this all about?" Geoff asked. "What're you guys talking about?"

"Nothing. Nothing at all. Just forget it! No problem at all," Aron said as he backed away from Buddy to attack the front right fender of his Honda.

"Aron, we did a terrible thing. Mario didn't do nothing to us. We should never have done that to him. It was two of us against that skinny little kid. We did a bad thing, Aron. I don't know what to do. I can't think of nothing else." Buddy continued to tremble, his voice evincing the strength of the emotions that were wracking him. "I was so scared when I heard about Mario today. He's dead, Aron. And I think that we did it..."

"You shut your fucking mouth. We didn't do nothing. He's dead? Well, he was alive when we left Los Lobos. So it's not my problem if he can't survive on his own. No skin off my nose!" Aron continued to apply wax to the hood of the Honda as he spoke. But his shoulders had noticeably tensed. The muscles of his back and shoulders and upper arms were flexed even when he wasn't applying the wax. He did not turn to his two friends as he spoke.

"Jesus Christ, Aron, what's Buddy saying?" Geoff interjected. You guys are the ones who tied him up? Shit! Why did you do that? He's a stupid, harmless kid!"

"Was, pal, *was*." Aron said quietly. "He was also a *spic*. So he shoulda known that he was in the wrong place. I already told him, '*Spics* don't surf Los Lobos.' He shoulda listened to me."

"Jesus, Aron! I can't believe what I'm hearing. What did you guys do?"

Aron turned and walked back toward the garage. "Come on, you guys. Let's just sit back here and talk. I got a couple of beers in the ice chest back here." As he entered the garage, he didn't bother to look back to see if Geoff and Buddy were following. They were, Geoff striding along to catch up to Aron, Buddy holding back, walking slowly.

Aron cracked open the three cans of beer and passed them to Geoff and Buddy. Geoff took his and sucked down a healthy swig. Buddy, seemingly unable to speak, shook his head and declined the offer. Aron leaned against the workbench in the garage; Geoff sat on an upturned wooden crate that was serving as a sawhorse for a surfboard that was in the process of being refinished. Buddy stood apart from either of his friends.

"Okay," Aron began. "Let's get this straight. We

didn't really do all that much wrong. We're not responsible for what happened to the *spic* after we left. And, anyway, there's no way they can pin anything on us. No evidence. Yeah, the fucking sheriff's got my bungee cord, but so what? You can't get no finger prints from a bungee cord!"

Buddy, having turned away from Aron's words, had been watching the street for several minutes. "Who're those guys stopped in the street out there, Aron? It's that *same* red Bronco. Like the one those guys were in when we were at *Mom and Pops* the other day. Remember? The one big guy who knocked your lunch out of your hands?"

"Those guys. Yeah, they've cruised by a couple of times today...yesterday, too. Fuck 'em! They're just a couple of faggoty-spics who think they're tough. Forget 'em." Aron moved to the front of the garage to stare in the direction of the Bronco. "Screw 'em!"

All three young men moved to the entry of the garage to watch as the Bronco made a u-turn in front of the house and then slowly moved on down the street. The tinted windows made it difficult for them to see just how many riders were in the vehicle.

"Anyway, think of it this way," Aron continued. "It's just one less kid who's gonna graduate from that stupid Engish-as-a-Second-Language crap." He laughed. "Jesus, you oughta hear my dad on the subject. "He always begins with the line, 'English is *not* a second goddamn language. And don't you forget it!' Then, he goes on and on about 'the power of the English language, the glory of the English language' and I always end up agreeing with him just to shut him up." Aron laughed again, and looked around at his two friends, and then finished off his beer. "But he's right, you know. They can't speak the language, they don't belong here. Period."

Geoff, finishing his beer, crushed the can and tossed it in the trash bin. "Yeah, well, we got to be going, Aron. I hope you're right!" he said hesitantly, pausing before asking, "We still on for tonight?"

"You bet!" Aron answered quickly. Maybe around 8:00. My parents will be gone by then. We can have a few beers and get cracking on finishing up sanding this here board. Maybe we can even get another coat of resin down, too."

Geoff and Buddy walked quickly to Geoff's car. Geoff turned to smile at his friend. "Well, if you ain't worried, then I'm not!"

Aron watched them leave. A worried expression crossed his face and told all. He thought to himself as Geoff pulled a u-turn in the street, *If that fucking Buddy spills his guts, we're in big trouble. He'd better keep that wuss mouth of his shut!*

"One problem," Geoff said to Buddy as they headed back down the hill into town. "I'm an aide in the ESL classes. Mario's not ESL. What do you think about that, Buddy?"

XXII

Wednesday evening, the weather continued, spring-time balmy, cloudless, windless, a picture postcard of California's beautiful central coast. Chris picked Reeni up at 7:15. They were on their way to the Rosary for Mario, and neither felt much like talking. Their "Hi's" just about summed up their moods. Chris drove on in silence, wondering what Alfredo was thinking right now, how he was going to handle the evening.

"I don't know if I could handle this, if I were Fredo," he said at last, staring straight ahead. She put her hand on his upper arm and smiled gently. "No. I can't imagine losing someone in my family. I never think about Mama or Daddy dying. I guess I simply don't want to..." Reeni's words trailed off in the silence that held sway in Chris' Toyota truck. She squeezed tenderly on his arm.

A few moments later, Chris looked over at her and

smiled. "Yeah...I guess it's something that we don't think will ever happen...so, when it does, well, I guess we haven't quite got ourselves together enough. Mario's gone. That's real. And that's hard to take. I wish now that I stood up for him and Alfredo better last Sunday. I didn't. And I'm hating myself for being such a chicken. I should have said something."

They rode together in silence for a few more minutes before Chris continued his thoughts. "I just can't understand how I could have been so blind. I mean, I knew about his temper. I guess I even knew about his problems with Mexicans. I just didn't pay much attention. It just didn't seem to be a problem for me! And now, I'm thinking *Could he really have done that to Mario? Is he really capable of tying someone down and leaving them like that? All night?* How could I have been so stupid!"

Reeni moved over closer to Chris and kissed him on his cheek. "Don't do this. Aron had me fooled, too. And anyway, we don't know what happened. If it was Aron, it certainly wasn't your fault. You can't take on this guilt – it's not yours!" Chris nodded and smiled gently, but didn't reply.

Moments later, Chris pulled into the gravel parking lot adjacent to San Marcos Mission, where there were already several dozen cars parked. People were gathering in small groups and walking across the bridge which led to the Mission's church. Chris slid out of his seat onto the gravel and Reeni slid across and followed Chris out of the driver's side. Together, holding hands tightly, they too crossed the bridge and walked slowly toward the big wooden double doors that marked the entrance to the vestibule of the church.

Alfredo came quickly down the steps as he saw them approach. He was followed by a petite, dark-haired, dark-eyed young woman in a long darkly-patterned skirt and blouse; she wore a black mantilla draped across her shoulders and over the back of her head. Alfredo smiled quietly as he came forward and embraced first Chris, then Reeni. "I'm glad you could come," he said. "There's gonna be a lot of people here. I'm going to need someone to fall back on. You're both my goat. I hope you don't mind!"

"Hey, we're here! So just use us, whatever!" Chris said, smiling back. "What say after this is over, we get something to eat...Just to get away!"

"Actually...Carlitos has already got that plan in mind," Alfredo answered. He paused momentarily, glancing at the young woman who stood silently by his side. "Dang! I'm sorry. Chris, Reeni, this is my girlfriend, Elisabeth Moreno. Liz, this is Chris Battleson and Reeni...uh, dang! Reeni...I'm sorry, I've forgotten your last name *again*!"

Reeni, smiling at Liz, said, "I'm Reeni Richter...and," looking at Alfredo, said, "don't worry about it, Alfredo, you've got a whole lot of other things on your mind!"

Chris and Liz shook hands, Chris saying, 'Nice to meet you Liz. Alfredo's pretty lucky, but then, so are you, I think!"

"Yes, I know. We have known each other for several years. We are both very lucky, I think. And from what Alfredo has told me, Reeni is pretty lucky herself!" The pause in their conversation was covered when Liz took Alfredo by the arm, saying, "We had probably better go inside now. They are going to be starting."

Alfredo smiled down at her and took her hand. "Yes. I guess so. I'll be glad when this is all over. Meanwhile, Chris, we're on for *the Villager* afterwards, right?"

Chris, taking Reeni's hand in his own again, nodded. "No problem! We'll be out here waiting for you guys." He and Reeni followed Alfredo into the vestibule of the Mission Church. Seats had been placed in rows down the apse, allowing for a central aisle, for early missions did not have pews for their penitents. Mourners had taken many of the folding chairs; others preferred to stand along the walls and at the back of the church. Chris looked around, noting that many of Mario's school mates from Mission High were in the seats as were a number of the Alhambras' family and friends.

He also noted and nudged Reeni, pointing out Mr. and Mrs. Levin. He wondered, *Did Aron choose not to come? Did Aron even know they were here?* He decided that Aron probably did not—or did not care. The casket, adorned with a simple spray of gladiolas and spring lilies, was placed just outside the communion rail in front of the altar. The altar itself was lit with candelabras across the back and three standing candles on each side of the casket. Sconces with lighted candles illuminated the side walls and floor of the church.

Two altar boys, one carrying a candle, the other carrying a tall, gilded crucifix, began a procession up the central aisle followed by three priests and two Franciscan brothers. Chris recognized Father Miguel from the hospital yesterday, and assumed the brothers were a part of the Mission parish as was the second priest whom he did not know. The third priest surprised Chris. It was Father Leo who, seeing Chris, nodded and smiled quietly in his direction. The Alhambra-Alvarez family, Alfredo and Liz and his parents, Carlos and his parents followed the priests.

The Rosary began with Father Miguel leading the parishioners in the *Apostles Creed*. A singer, who moved from the sidewall of the church to a side of the altar, began to quietly strum a guitar. The notes were slow and somber and floated across the church proper even as the priests continued with the Rosary, each priest and the two brothers praying a Mystery.

As the prayers ended, the guitarist began *Ave Maria*, singing the Latin words known throughout the world, *gratia plena...* As he concluded and began to play another melody, the altar boys led the procession of priests and Franciscan brothers back down the central aisle, followed by the Alhambra-Alvarez families. They walked slowly, the parents holding hands; the two young men, Alfredo and Carlitos, following their parents, walked rigidly, shoulder to shoulder. Chris watched as Liz joined her parents and followed the families out of the church.

Outside of the Mission, Chris and Reeni waited quietly at the bottom of the steps. They watched as Alfredo and Carlitos talked quietly with one another and, as the occasion arose, greeted mourners who came up to give their condolences. At one time, Alfredo looked over at Chris, grimaced and then smiled. Finally, as Liz came up to Alfredo and took his arm, he and Carlitos quietly disengaged themselves from the families and walked toward Chris and Reeni. As Chris watched, Alfredo halted suddenly and looked back at his father. He was shaking hands and talking with another man, a man

Alfredo had only heard the name of, a man Chris knew as Aron's father, Benjamin Levin. Alfredo stared momentarily at this gentleman who seemed to be commiserating with his father.

Still glancing backward, Alfredo strode toward Chris and Reeni. As he drew near, he said quietly to Chris, "Do you know who that guy is, right there, talking to Daddy? That's Mr. —"

"Yeah, I know," Chris interrupted. "He's Aron's dad. He's the City Attorney. Your dad and him—they're business associates. So he probably thought he should be here. Anyway, he probably doesn't know all of what is coming down! So, Alfredo, just shake it off! It's gonna be all right!"

"Okay...You're right. I just now put it together! Levin...Aron *Levin*! Shit!" He paused, shaking his head in disbelief. "I say we just get out of here!" Alfredo continued, beginning to smile. "Liz and I will ride with Carlitos in his Bronco. We'll meet you guys up at *The Villager*."

"Sure!" Chris answered. "Where're you parked? Out there, or did you guys get some special passes?" He paused, laughing, "Just kidding!"

"Nah. We're just poor Mexicans! Remember? No special passes, today!" Alfredo laughed and covertly flipped Chris the finger before he began walking toward the parked cars. "I think I'm going to make it after all," he murmured to Liz.

XXIII

Geoff and Buddy pulled up to the curb in front of Aron Levin's home. Its brick and redwood ranch-style front was impressive for its clean lines and immaculate landscaping. Flowering borders led up the flagstone front walk, miniature citrus trees flanked the flagstone front porch which extended the length of the front of the house. Hanging baskets of perennially blooming begonias were suspended from the overhanging eaves. Birch trees in small copses dotted the wide expanse of front lawn. Landscape lighting illuminated the white bark of the trees and cast graceful shadows across the lawn. Mr. Levin, it seemed, was particularly proud of his home and paid well to have it manicured bi-weekly. Leaves simply were not a welcome addition to the lawns and walkways.

Geoff and Buddy could see from the curbside that

Aron was already at work on the surfboard. The lights in the garage and along the curved driveway clearly illuminated him bent over the board with his palm sander. Geoff pulled his own palm sander out of the trunk of his Chevy El Camino and handed Buddy an extra one that he had brought along.

"Hey, Aron. I thought you said about eight!" Geoff called as they came up the drive.

"Yeah, well, Dad and Mother left early. They didn't say, but I think that they went to that kid's funeral service. Dad works with the *spic's* father, apparently," Aron answered without turning around. "So I thought I'd just get crackin' on this puppy!" He was still shirtless in the balmy evening. Sweat was beading on his neck and back and dripping off his dark hair.

Both Geoff and Buddy had changed into what would rightly be called their "work-clothes": Cut-offs, tank tops, flip-flops. As they approached the garage door, Aron turned off his sander and reached into a cooler where he had stashed two six-packs of beer and a bucket of ice. He withdrew two and tossed them to Geoff and Buddy as they approached. "Here!" he said, "and let's get a plan going here. This is what I've been thinking. We're almost finished with the bottom of the board. Geoff, you help with your sander; Buddy, you follow him and me with the hand sanding. There's some fine-grade sandpaper there on the bench. Okay with you guys?"

Geoff nodded and reached for the extra extension cord on the bench to plug in his palm sander. "Okay. But before we begin...you sure about what you guys did to that Mexican kid? I mean—"

"Hey, Geoff, lighten up! It's not a problem. We're in

the clear. So let's not sweat the small stuff!" Aron said, smiling at his two friends. "Let's get started. The board's pretty much finished, I think. I did some finish-sanding this afternoon. You can check it out when we get this sanded," Aron answered. His confidence relayed itself to Geoff who also stripped off his tank top and reached for his beer.

Aron took a long swig from his beer can and watched Geoff as he popped the top of his and took a quick drink. "You not drinking tonight, Buddy?" he asked.

"Yeah. I'm drinking..." Buddy said defensively. Nonetheless, he paused before he too popped his can. He didn't take a drink. He merely set the can on the workbench and carefully chose a sheet from among the various grades of sandpaper. He waited to be told where he could start. Geoff looked over at Aron who was watching Buddy closely.

"Buddy. Why don't you start at the tip. It looks like that end of the board is ready for finish-sanding," Geoff said, more to break the uneasy silence that had suddenly fallen on the garage.

Soon all three young men were busy, bending over the two humming palm sanders gliding over the surface of the board. Buddy, his back to the garage door, was intent on finish-sanding, running his hand over the surface every few moments to be sure that it was smooth, ready for another coat of resin. No one of the young men noticed the three visitors until the leader, known as Manuel, stepped into the driveway lights over the garage and cast a shadow over the surf board. All three jerked their heads toward the garage door, palm sanders suddenly quiet. They watched as the three visitors entered the garage, pulling gloves over their hands as they did so.

"Good evening, *senors!*" Manuel said. He was tall, dark-skinned, brawny. He was one of the two who had accompanied Carlos to confront Aron at *The Villager* last Monday at lunch. Another one moved to stand immediately behind Manuel. All three young men recognized these two; the third visitor, who hung back, they didn't know.

"You want to shut the doors, Mike," Manuel said as he stepped further into the garage. The other two visitors followed him into the interior; the second one, Mike, moved to close the garage doors after them.

"What do you guys want, dude?" Aron asked stepping aggressively forward. He clutched the palm sander in his hand as if it had suddenly become his weapon of choice. "This is private property you're standing on, assholes. You'd better have a goddamned good reason to be trespassing! And just who the fuck said you could close the door!?!"

"Hey, Mike, Jaime," Manuel said over his shoulder. "You guys hear that? We're *trespassing!*" He spat out the words, laughing as he did so, and moved rapidly to stand within inches of Aron's face. "Get your ass back against the wall," he said, and the menace in his tone left no doubt as to his meaning. He reached across the inches and shoved Aron violently backwards. Aron stumbled, nearly fell, then caught himself, even as he struck the side wall of the garage.

"You two..." he said fingering both Geoff and Buddy. "Get down on the ground. Yeah, that's right. Just sit there on the floor against the bench, *camaradas*. We'll get to you in a minute." Geoff and Buddy quietly slid to the floor at the base of the work bench. Buddy dropped his head to rest on his knees.

The other two, Mike and Jaime, moved quickly around the surf board, Mike picking the board up as he did so. Handling it as if it were a stick of balsa, he shoved it viciously into Aron's body. The board's sharp impact knocked Aron's breath away and opened a gash across his forehead. Aron caught his breath, gasping and pushing the surf board aside, and raised the palm sander as if to hit his attacker. The sander dropped from his hand as Jaime chopped brutally with the side of his hand across Aron's wrist. The board fell to the garage floor at the feet of Buddy and Geoff.

Mike, looking at Aron who was bent double trying to catch his breath, laughed lightly and said, "Manny, is this fun, or what! The little punk's gonna start to cry, I think."

Manuel waited silently, watching the actions of his partner. Nodding at Mike, he smiled at Aron, saying, "Hey, *amigo*, you got a little blood on your face! I tell you what, you lie down here and maybe, just maybe, the blood'll stop!" And stepping toward Aron, he swiftly kicked at Aron's ankles, knocking his legs out from under him. Aron fell heavily to the floor and rolled over onto his stomach, sprawled across the board.

"Noooo, *amigo*. That's not how we want it!" Manuel said soothingly. He kicked Aron again, this time in the ribs. "We want you *on* the surf board. *Just like Mario.* Now roll over, get your ass onto the surf board, face up, dirtbag. Just like Mario on Monday night! You remember Monday night?" And for a third time in less than a minute, he kicked at Aron, this time in the temple. Aron moaned, but did not cry out. He raised his head slightly, looked for and found the surf board. Moaning still, he inched his body around it, crawling on top of the board to lie on his back. He breathed heavily and with some obvious difficulty.

"Now, that's *bueno*! You recognize the position, *amigo*? You should! *Remember Mario*? All we need now are a couple of bungee cords. You got any to spare, *amigo*?" He paused and looked about him. "Well, what do you think, Mike?" he said looking over at his partner. Again he smiled when he heard Mike's quiet laughter.

Jaime, the third member of the visiting team, spoke for the first time. "You know what, Manny? I don't think this dude's gonna go anywhere. Bungee cords be a waste."

"Yeah, you're right, Jaime. Be a waste of time and effort. Plus, we'd have to touch his *gringo* body. Look at him sweat! We want *to touch* him? No cords. Okay with you Mike?" Manuel paused and looked over to see Mike, nodding in agreement. "Good. Then, let's deal with these two *gringos*. You guys friends with this Aron Levin guy?" Manuel had moved to stand directly above Geoff and Buddy who remained sitting on the floor. Both nodded, but did not speak.

"I cannot hear you, *amigos*. You gotta speak up. I ask again: You creeps know this asshole?"

Geoff, sitting upright, spoke first. "Yeah, we know him," he said aggressively. "Whatta think we're doing here?"

"Ooooh. I don't much like your tone, *amigo*," Manuel said. He looked toward Mike, and Mike stretched out his foot and brutally kicked Geoff in the stomach with the toe of his boot. Geoff reacted with an audible gasp and bent double with the pain of the blow.

Buddy began quietly to cry, tears staining his face. "Well, little *amigo*. Lookie here, Jaime, we do got us a *muchacho*...who cries!" Manuel laughed. He reached down and patted Buddy twice on his left cheek before slapping him powerfully. Buddy's head jerked to his right shoulder in reaction to the blow.

Mike, watching this play out, moved up to Manuel's side. "We'd better be getting on with this show, Manny. We're running a little late." He pulled his Smith and Wesson *LS60* from his pocket. "You like this, Manny? It's my newest toy! Small, ain't it. But no sweat, it'll do the job!"

Manuel looked at each of the three young men in turn. First at Buddy, whose head had slumped to his chest; then to Geoff who, having straightened up, stared off into the space directly in front of him. He would not look at his attackers. And finally, Manuel paused to stare at Aron who lay quietly on the surf board, his face a blotch of wet blood, much of which had seeped into his eyes. Aron could see nothing. Shirtless, his chest, smeared with blood, heaved as he tried to contain the fear that had taken control of his being.

"Yeah, let's get on with it, Mike," Manuel said, returning his gaze to the two young men seated on the floor in front of him. "Just so you guys know, *this is for Mario...for what you did to Mario*. You dirt-bags left our brother to die on the beach. You don't deserve to live." Manuel nodded to Mike who calmly pulled his revolver up first to Buddy's temple and then to Geoff's. He fired twice. The silencer attached to his weapon muted the shots.

"Good. Now this one's mine," Manuel said, moving to stand directly in front on Aron. He unbuttoned his coat, revealing the Heckler and Koch *MP7A1* shotgun nested in the holster at his waist band. "Maybe he'll have some time to suffer before he packs it in. You think?" Mike nodded and Jaime laughed quietly. "Yeah, he needs to remember our Mario for a last few minutes."

Manuel nodded; he pulled the shotgun from its holster, adjusting its length and snapping the sound suppressor onto the barrel; he stepped back several feet from the figure lying on the surfboard. Taking aim carefully, he fired at Aron, first in the stomach, and again in the chest. The scatter pattern of the shells sprayed bits of torn flesh and blood into the air.

The three visitors prudently flicked off the lights to the garage and driveway on their way out the door. Pulling off their gloves and stuffing them into their coat pockets, they walked quickly to their car which had been parked on the street several doors up from the Levins' home. Checking to see if they had been noticed by neighbors, they slid into the seats of their Chevy pickup and drove quietly away. No outside lights had gone on in neighborhood, no suspicious neighbors had appeared at their doors or in their driveways. Neighbors often don't see or hear those things they don't want to see or hear in their neighborhood.

XXIV

It was already getting on into the evening, when Chris and Reeni pulled into the parking lot of the *Villager.* Alfredo and Liz had arrived minutes earlier and were standing alongside the red Bronco. Carlos was at the open rear cargo door. He pulled out a red and yellow knapsack and reached inside for his wallet, at the same time checking his watch. Alfredo and Liz met Chris and Reeni across the parking lot, greeting each other genially. All five stood in line to order, the two young women ordering hot tea and English muffins; Chris and Alfredo, hamburgers and cokes; Carlos, coffee.

Each of the young men carried a tray to one of the outer cement tables with its quarter-round benches. Seated there, they were somewhat apart from the few other customers at the *Mom and Pop's*, yet still close in and away from the parking lot. Their view was of the mesa and its grasslands and scrub oaks awash in the moonlight, and of the highway leading in one direction into town and Dos Padres High School and in the other direction toward the homes that surrounded the Mission High. Farther on, up the same stretch lay the Ranch Estates and Sunset Ranch.

Their desultory conversation ranged from their classes at Mission to Liz's classes at Dos Padres. Reeni buttering lightly her muffin, engaged Liz in conversation about their plans after high school. Chris again asked Alfredo about his art work: did he frame any pictures? did he ever consider showing his work? would Alfredo let him see some of them sometime?

Alfredo, finishing off his hamburger, was self-denigrating for his part, answered "some," and "no" and laughingly acknowledging that "yes," a few of them he *had* framed, but that framing them was mostly a kind of "ego-boosting exercise"; that art, as a whole, just gave him "an outlet from school work and day-to-day *crap*." He smiled across at Chris and agreed, finally, that "yes," Chris could see them on the condition that he, Chris, "wouldn't laugh" at his efforts.

Carlos, sipping at his coffee, did not enter the conversation until Chris, both having an ulterior motive as well as recognizing an opportunity to bring him in asked him about his work on the ranch. He shrugged off his supervision of the cattle and horses, until Alfredo interrupted him, saying, "Carlitos, you *run* the whole friggin' operation! Dang, man!"

Chris jumped at this opening, the one that he was waiting for, and said, "Carlos, what are the chances that I could get hired on with you after graduation? I've never worked a ranch before, but I think I could learn the ropes pretty quickly. And, starting right after graduation, I'm gonna be looking for a full-time job for a couple of years I'm pretty strong and used to hard work!"

"That's not a bad idea, Carlitos" Alfredo interjected.

However, this line of conversation was suddenly and abruptly interrupted by the air-splitting sounds of wailing sirens on the highway adjacent to the *Villager*. The sirens were almost immediately followed by the flashing of emergency lights as two EMT wagons and several sheriff's vehicles and a fire truck raced by.

"Dang! Those guys are hauling ass!" Alfredo said.

"They're going up to the mesa. I wonder what that's all about!" Reeni replied.

"I don't know, but they sure aren't wasting any time getting to wherever they're going!" Alfredo answered. "I guess somebody—or maybe, some *people* are in big trouble. *Two* EMTs…that looks pretty grim, if you ask me."

Carlos watched the vehicles pass, but did not offer up any opinions of his own. He merely sat there, watching and listening. He smiled slightly when he heard his cousin describe the situation as *grim*. He nodded to Alfredo, but still remained silent.

The sudden appearance of so many emergency vehicles seemed to cast a kind of pall over the five young people. Conversation dwindled, and they decided, almost simultaneously, that it was time to call it a night.

"It's been a long couple days, Alfredo concluded. "And tomorrow," he continued quietly to Liz, "is going to be another day."

Getting up from the table, they bused their plates and

cups. Chris and Reeni warmly said their goodnights to Liz, and Chris said that he hoped to see Alfredo at school tomorrow at first period.

Alfredo, suddenly turning serious, said, "No, Chris. Not tomorrow. That's Mario's funeral. It's a private one. Just us family. We figured the Rosary was good enough for the folks we know, but we need the funeral to be just us. I'll catch you afterwards...maybe we can go surfing tomorrow afternoon late?

Chris laughed. "Yeah...That would be cool, Fredo. Very cool. Call me. Tomorrow's on at Los Lobos. Oh, boy!"

"Yeah, right, just you and your Mex-friend surfing Los Lobos," Alfredo said, chuckling.

They left laughing. The irony was not lost on anyone. Even Carlos grinned.

XXV

Special to the Dos Padres Sun Times
by Eric Ramos, Staff Writer

Dos Padres Valley police have increased patrols in the Ranch District after a series of violent murders last night claimed the lives of three of the Valley's prominent teenagers.

The victims, identified as Aron Levin, Geoff Bradley and Raymond (Buddy) Johnson, were discovered brutally murdered in the garage of the Levin family home late in the evening after Aron's parents returned home around nine-thirty.

While details of the murders remain sketchy as of this morning, Inspector Karen Michaels of the homicide detail said that police responded to the

911 call from Mr. Levin, father of Aron, who discovered the three young men lying in pools of blood in the garage of his home.

Two of the young men had been shot once in the head in what appeared, Ms Michaels reported, as "execution style." Both were dead when the police arrived on the scene.

A third young man, who had been shot two times, once in the stomach and once in the chest with what appeared to be a small gauge shot gun, was unconscious when police arrived and died en route to the hospital.

Curiously, Ms Michaels reported, the shot-gun victim was lying face up on a surfboard that the victims had apparently been working on when attacked.

The police reportedly have no suspects at this time. Relatives of the three boys are quoted as saying that the three were friendly, active seniors at Mission High School. All three were considered popular and had no known enemies.

According to young Levin's aunt, "This was a senseless act of violence. All Aron did was work hard in school, be a friend to his classmates...This is a tragedy, a terrible tragedy, that shouldn't have happened," she was quoted as saying.

Printed in the United States
64705LVS00002B/337